DEATH BY HONEYMOON

Book #1 in the Caribbean Murder series

Jaden Skye

ISBN: 978-0-9765855-0-3

Chapter 1

Finally, there was nothing to fear. The wedding was over, he was hers, and their honeymoon so far was all she'd ever dreamt of. Lying beside him on a blanket on the white Caribbean sands, surrounded by the beauty of the turquoise waters, she exhaled.

Nothing could have prepared her for the unbelievable beauty of this place. The beach was surrounded by palm trees, winding roads and hidden birds. Some of them sang intermittently as the waves rolled up onto the shore. It had power to heal the upset she'd gone through. No one had been able to stop their wedding from happening, although his family had tried.

Clint moved closer. She could smell his suntan lotion, mixed with salt from the ocean. He took her slender hand and his rugged strength rose up through her, as she turned to him and smiled. It was a smile of contentment. Of Victory. Cindy had won. She'd fought hard for this marriage, and nothing could take it away.

As if reading her thoughts, Clint whispered in her ear, "We did it. We're together now, forever. Everything else is in the past."

Cindy took a deep breath. She'd always been afraid to believe in forever, but now she could. Her relationship with Clint was soothing her mind. Her own father had died when she was a little girl and it had been a long time before she'd been willing to trust life again. With Clint beside her, she could.

Cindy watched the sun glistening on the waves, rising faster and faster. High tide was coming in. The surf here was fed by swirling currents from the Atlantic Ocean, pouring into the cove. The sound of the waves, crashing on the rocks, startled her for a moment. This place was perfect for Clint. He was an avid surfer, craved the ocean, and required challenge. This beach was off the beaten course, wild, untamed, not the usual destination for travelers. It was famous for its wild surf.

"It will make our honeymoon even more thrilling," he'd said, when he suggested this spot. There were milder turfs nearby, where she could surf as well. But Cindy wanted it to be the honeymoon of his dreams. It didn't matter to her that most couples went to the comfortable West Side of Barbados, while they headed East to the rugged shore.

"Where did you say you were going?" the driver that picked them up from the airport had asked twice .

"El Barado Hotel," Clint had repeated.

The driver had looked at them, skeptical. "You know where you're going? You're going to the *real* Barbados. You're sure?"

"Very sure," Clint grinned.

"Ok." Then the car had sped away from the airport, turning off the main road.

Cindy was proud of Clint. He was so sure of everything. He wasn't one to take old, tired familiar pathways. Cindy loved that about him. He reminded her of what was possible. She used to be strong and confident like that. His words brought her back to herself.

As their car had wound its way further and further, Cindy realized they were heading somewhere out of the ordinary. They wound through country lanes, past sugar cane farms and quaint villages made up of small single-story houses. There were food shacks along the roads and simple clapboard churches. It was clearly where the locals lived and worked.

Their car had driven quickly through the villages, and right up to the hotel. It seemed to be rushing, as if there weren't a minute to lose.

"There it is," the driver had pointed.

The hotel came into view, sprawled behind rocks, at the edge of the beach, looking out at the ocean. "Not too many people know about this place."

The outside of the hotel was trimmed with wraparound plantation shutters, brass hanging lamps and hurricane lights. Clint had found out about it from some executives at his company, who were also rabid surfers, like him. They loved Clint. As a wedding present, the company offered to pay part of the expenses.

He was thrilled. Cindy and Clint had tipped the driver generously, as he'd brought their bags up to the front door.

Alex, a grinning local, hefty man in his fifties, greeted them.

"Welcome to the Island," he'd said in a lilting tone. "We are happy to have you here. Our honeymoon guests are our favorites. Congratulations."

Cindy felt warm inside as she'd entered. She'd looked through the large windows in the lobby, overlooking the ocean, and saw miles of rolling waves. She knew Clint would see that and have an overwhelming urge to surf.

Alex had patted Clint on the shoulder. "You a strong swimmer?" he'd asked.

Clint had grinned. A lifeguard when he was younger, that was his last concern. "It's what I came here for. Don't worry: I'm right where I belong." He always said that when he came to the ocean.

There was a lot to do. Scuba diving, snorkeling, visiting the island's indigenous turtles, photographing this incredible place.

They got a key and went right up to their room. It was open, airy, with salty breezes wafting in. There was a patio and a low-plank coffee table filled with seashells and sea urchins. Best of all, you could hear the waves, constantly crashing on the sand and rocks outside. They'd dropped their luggage, changed quickly and headed right down to the beach.

*

Day after day had been fantastic. They'd been snorkeling, swimming, dancing, having delicious dinners, and making love all night long. Laying here now on the sand with her new husband, Cindy felt as if she had been welcomed into a new phase of life. She put her head on Clint's shoulder.

These days of happiness had wiped away the pressures and worries they'd grown so accustomed to the past several months. His family's agitation and schemes drifted like smoke into the crystal blue sky. It hadn't been easy. There had been one obstacle after another.

Now the time was passing quickly. They had only two days left. Cindy's heart dropped at the thought of leaving.

"I don't want this to ever end," she'd said when they woke up that morning, before they got out of bed.

"It won't end," he'd answered softly. "We'll remember this forever."

"Do you promise?"

He'd laughed. "Of course."

"Don't promise something you can't keep," Cindy joked. She knew he was always good for his word.

"I promise," he repeated.

For no reason at all, her heart dropped. "But everything ends--"

"Not necessarily," he stroked her long, auburn hair, and kissed the freckles on her forehead. "We take our memories with us wherever we go."

It never occurred to Cindy that there was any possibility that they wouldn't actually leave the island in two days' time.

Or that, four days later, she would *still* be on the island—and cradling her husband's dead body in her arms.

Chapter 2

The day it happened was perfect. They woke up early to a cloudless day, nestled in each other's arms. They showered together and went downstairs for breakfast, laughing. It seemed that the whole world was at peace that day. As they ate breakfast out on the Veranda, they were serenaded by a throng of birds, flying in and out of the branches of the trees that surrounded the hotel.

"It must be the amazing weather," Clint had said, gazing at the water and sky. "Sky's so blue, air's so still, doesn't even seem as if there could be a ripple in the ocean." It was unusual weather for the island.

Over breakfast they talked about the souvenirs they were bringing home: huge, crusty sea shells, driftwood, throw cushions covered with tropical prints, photographs of whistling turtles, porpoises and flying fish . There was something for everyone.

As they lingered over coffee, Cindy knew the honeymoon was coming to an end. She began to think about going home, of the quaint, small starter home they'd bought back on Long

Island, New York. It was in a cove, near the end of a long, private road. They both loved the house the minute they saw it and were ecstatic when their offer was accepted.

"Soon, we'll be in our new home," Cindy had said. "Only two more days."

"There's a lot we can still cram in today," he said.

Clint planned their activities down to the minute, not wanting to waste a second. They were planning to go surfing together in the afternoon, and she'd made reservations for dinner at the hotel's main restaurant, under the palm trees, for eight o'clock. It would be a special dinner, the anniversary of the night they'd met.

As they ate, other guests came down, milled around and sat at tables near them. They all smiled at each other casually, giving each other the privacy they wanted . Pedro, their favorite waiter, hummed a local song as he brought them a platter of croissants, eggs, fruits, coffee and mimosas. He took special care that Cindy had just what she wanted. In fact, he'd made a special desert for her, a torte. Just the kind she loved and had ordered every day. "But today's is better," he'd said. Cindy had smiled. These were good people.

Cindy had looked at Clint and felt how grateful and fortunate she was. From very soon after she met him, she'd known he was the man she wanted to live her life with. Tall, rugged, handsome and determined, he was the most honest and caring man she'd ever met.

After breakfast, they'd had a tranquil, long morning walk on the beach, he looking out at the horizon and trying to memorize the view, and she gathering the occasional seashell. They'd then headed back to the room to change for surfing.

And as they went upstairs, that's when it hit her.

Cindy had suddenly began to feel woozy.

Probably from the sun, she'd thought, *especially after those mimosas.*

Then she had cramps.

They'll probably pass, she'd told herself, and had gone into the bathroom, where it was cooler. But the cramps got worse.

Clint was changing into his surfing gear, and another wave of dizziness overcame her as she'd held her stomach in pain. She lay down on the bed, hoping for it to pass.

Clint came over, surprised to see her laying there.

"What's going on?" he asked, concerned.

"I don't know…just cramps, I think. I feel like I need to take a nap."

"Now? In the middle of the afternoon?" he was surprised.

"I'm so sorry. I don't feel like I can go. I probably just need to rest. But don't let me stop you. I'll nap for an hour and then meet you down at the beach. I promise."

That seemed to cheer him. "Okay, but just for an hour," he said. "I don't want to be away from you for too long."

Cindy wanted to reach up and hug him, but a wave of exhaustion overcame her. Helpless against it, she closed her eyes, and the next thing she knew, she was asleep.

*

Cindy woke with a start. She knew it was late.

With a shock, she sat straight up in bed. The clock read 5 o'clock. She had slept for three hours.

She jumped out of bed, went to the sink and splashed cold water on her face. She'd told Clint she'd be down on the beach in an hour. She was two hours late. He was probably down on the sand, waiting for her.

Feeling badly, she threw on her new shorts and a shirt, grabbed her key, and then flew down the wooden staircase to the lobby.

Alex, behind the main desk, smiled and waved at her as she appeared. During these days he seemed to have taken a special liking to Cindy and Clint. He'd brought them coffee in the morning and kept asking if there was anything they needed to make everything perfect.

"You need anything, miss?" he called out to her again.

"No, thank you, thank you," Cindy said and rushed out of the hotel, down to the beach.

She hurried down the beach to the spot where she and Clint were supposed to meet, expecting to see him there, waiting for her. The sun was setting, and the temperature had dropped, and she realized that he must have been waiting for her for hours. He was probably disappointed. They'd only had two days left on the honeymoon, and she had promised to surf with him. She could already picture his expression of frustration.

She doubled her pace, taking off her sandals and carrying them, and as she turned the bend, she was surprised.

The beach was empty.

She stopped and looked around, in every direction. He had to be somewhere. Had he laid down on the sand, under a palm tree, maybe?

But she surveyed the trees closely, and there was no one. All of the hammocks were empty. Of course they were: it was getting dark and cold, and the wind was blowing them wildly.

Maybe Clint had taken a walk along the shore? She ran to the water's edge, and looked up and down.

But there was no one in sight.

She took out her cell and checked it again. No new messages.

Her heart started to pound, as panic overcame her. She walked quickly down the shoreline, looking every which way.

She looked out at the ocean and noticed there was a strong sideways current. Maybe it had taken him along the beach, like it sometimes did, and he hadn't even realized. That must be it.

She followed the current sideways, along the beach, increasing her pace with every step.

But still, nothing. The beach was oddly empty. Not one person was there.

A wave of fear suddenly washed over her, and she started to run, to sprint mindlessly down the beach, staring out at the water.

Out of breath, she finally stopped running, and took a deep, wet, salty breath. In the last few minutes the sky had suddenly darkened, and the wind had picked up, becoming much stronger, nearly knocking her off balance. The wind whipped her hair into her face and eyes. She struggled to pull it away.

"Clint!" she screamed, her voice quickly drowned out by the thunderous waves. "Where are you!?"

And then, as she looked up, she saw it. In the distance, something in the water.

She ran towards it, and as she got closer, she saw what it was.

Clint's blue surfboard. Floating in the waves.

And Clint nowhere in sight.

Her hands got clammy and her heart pounded, as a wave of horror engulfed her. There was no way, there was absolutely no way, that Clint would have ever left his board.

The ferocious waves, rougher than usual, smashed into each other mercilessly, tossing his surfboard every which way.

A strange bird flew overhead, screeching.

And at that moment, Cindy knew in every bone of her body that her husband was dead .

Chapter 3

One week later

The days were a blur. Cindy had no idea how she'd managed to get back home. A thick fog descended over her, and she moved about as if in a dream. She moved slowly, her limbs frozen and numb. Everything seemed surreal. She was frozen in time, in a nightmare she couldn't get out of.

From time to time the fog lifted and she heard herself sobbing.

This can't be happening. It's a dream. I'll wake up and he'll be here with me. Clint, you promised.

Then the fog returned and it was hard to remember anything.

During the first week at home, she mostly slept. She could hear the phone ringing off the hook—not just her cellphone, which she ignored, and finally shut off—but also the landline that Clint had installed in the house. It never seemed to stop. Her sister Ann had flown in from Wisconsin and was staying with her, and thankfully, she answered it for her.

In those first few days, Ann was her lifeline. An endless stream of visitors kept stopping by, and when Cindy refused to see them, Ann met them at the door and gently asked them to return another time.

Cindy's mother had called the first day, to say how sorry she was, and to say that she couldn't make it, that she had to keep running her art gallery, back home in Wisconsin. How typical of her, Cindy thought.

She tried to offer Cindy advice over the phone. "This will take time," she murmured. "Be patient. Little by little, you'll feel better."

Her words did not comfort Cindy at all. Would she ever feel better? Cindy doubted it. How dare she feel better when Clint was dead?

Clint's family, while they lived only a mile away, still hadn't come to visit. Cindy hoped they never would.

Ann kept insisting that she come out of the bedroom and greet people, and on the one day that Cindy finally relented, Ann helped her get out of bed. Then she gently guided her down the stairs, into the living room, and onto the marine-blue suede couch in the living room that she and Clint had just purchased. Clint had loved it because it reminded him of the ocean. Now it reminded her of the waves that had beaten him so brutally. She would have to get rid of it, she thought in passing, as she sat on it and shivered.

The guests who came to offer condolences didn't stay long. They seemed to be at a loss what to say. Many of them were the same guests who had been to their wedding a little over a week ago. Most were pale and ashen. They shook their heads in disbelief.

"He was so young," Moira mentioned, tears in their eyes. She was an old college friend of Clint's. "I can't believe this happened."

"He had everything ahead of him," one of Clint's mother's friends kept repeating.

There was an assortment of people, friends, co-workers, neighbors from down the road who Cindy and Clint had barely met.

Finally, Cindy had had enough. Without warning, she flew out of the living room.

Ann grabbed her arm in the kitchen. "What are you doing?" she asked, mortified.

"I've had enough!" Cindy screamed, breaking into tears. "I don't want to see anyone! I refuse!"

And with that, she'd stormed back up into her bedroom, leaving Ann to pick up the pieces—and hadn't left since. That was days ago.

Cindy lay there now, staring up at the ceiling, lost in thought. For the millionth time, she struggled to remember, to try to recall the events of the past days.

When they'd finally found his body after two days, washed up on the rocks, inside of a cove, crumpled, his head snapped, beaten by the surf, she'd felt herself die with him.

She had been called immediately to identify the body.

"It's not him," she said at first.

The local police looked at her strangely.

"That's not him," she repeated. "Clint is alive. He was stronger than any wave."

The police scratched a few words on a pad of paper.

"Does he look like him?" one of the cops asked quietly.

"It's Clint's body," she started yelling. "But it's not Clint. I know him. I love him. He would never have let this happen."

*

There had been a full out search for him on the island when he didn't show up at the hotel that night. Cindy remembered a wild rush of phone calls between the States and the island. Her family couldn't get a flight. Two top executives at Clint's firm got involved. There were calls to officials on the island. The firm was well connected and sent down people on a company jet to help with the search. Some of them suggested that she return home. This could take weeks, they said, even months. They would cover all bases.

Cindy refused to leave without Clint. She spent every moment staring at the ocean, praying. Even though she begged for Clint to be saved, deep within she knew it was too late.

She lost all track of time. It was as if lifetimes passed as she sat without moving, gazing at the sky.

But to everyone's amazement, it was only two days until they found him, his body washed up on shore.

"A stroke of luck," she heard one official say. A tall guy with a moustache and squinty eyes.

What kind of luck? Cindy wondered.

"Yeah," the other official, a shorter, squat guy, agreed. "These kinds of searches can go on for years with nothing to show for it. Usually the ocean takes them out and under. Who finds a body here?"

They both shrugged and looked at each other. Cindy's stomach clenched. She imagined Clint being taken out and under by the unforgiving ocean, dragged into oblivion, with nothing left behind. Should she consider herself lucky that they'd found his body?

The police had called someone from Clint's firm in to identify the body as well. Henry Greerson. He'd been sent down by the firm to oversee everything and make sure Cindy was well cared for. Cindy had met him once or twice before. She never much liked him. He was a middle-aged guy in a button down suit who seemed cold and withdrawn around her. Clint had liked him, though. They'd worked together on several projects. Clint said he was a good man. Clint said that about everyone, or almost everyone. If he liked you, he loved you.

Greerson immediately identified the body. Soon after, the death was declared accidental. Strong turf, sudden riptide. These riptides happened all the time on the East Shore of Barbados.

Cindy remembered Greerson escorting her home on the plane, along with the remains. The two of them didn't talk to each other. She had nothing to say, and neither did he. At least he respected her need for silence, and probably realized she was in shock.

*

Cindy spent the first days back mostly curled up in bed. Ann didn't intrude. She only helped Cindy come out of the bedroom when guests appeared. Otherwise, she brought her food in on a tray, and put soft music on the CD player. Ann had always been the most wonderful older sister anyone could have ever wanted. Her husband, Frank, told her to stay as long as she was needed. They had a lovely marriage. It seemed that things always went smoothly in Ann's life. Cindy never felt she could quite live up to her.

Cindy's relationships with guys growing up was always short and fitful. She was always afraid they would leave, the way her father had.

She had a few good friends, but became quite bookish, preferring her time alone, studying, doing research, gathering all kinds of information for papers she wrote, sketching and making collages. . Ann was always there, watching over her, worrying about Cindy all her years growing up.

When Cindy met Clint, everything seemed to change. She'd become happy, secure, confident. She left the house freely, went new places with him, laughed a lot, seemed like a different person. Her sister Ann told her she didn't trust the relationship, though she didn't know why. Now it was as if an old premonition of Ann's had come true. It was clear how worried Ann was about what would become of Cindy now.

Slowly Cindy began to emerge from the bedroom. She felt claustrophobic in there, dreaming of Clint almost every day. In the dreams, he looked real, completely alive. He was standing on his surfboard, waving at her, trying to speak.

But she couldn't make out what he was saying. The surf was too rough, too loud. It got in the way. She waved back, but couldn't reach him. Then the wave pulled him back out and took him away.

She woke with a start every time.

"He's trying to reach me," Cindy kept telling her sister.

Ann didn't say much in return.

"I know he is," Cindy insisted. "In my dream, his mouth is open and he's trying to talk. I can't hear him."

"They are just dreams," Ann finally said, softly. "He's gone, Cindy. It's you who wants to see him again. Those are *your* wishes."

Cindy was frustrated. Her dreams felt like more than wishes. She was going to say something else, but Ann interrupted, "It takes time for a person to absorb a shock like this. It takes time for it to feel real."

Ann always had something sensible to say, but this time Cindy didn't want to hear it. What happened to Clint wasn't sensible—it didn't make sense at all. She had seen Clint surf in much rougher waters than that. She couldn't fathom how he could have drowned.

Cindy thought of all the plans she and Clint had had for the future. Just being in the house brought them all back. She looked at the photographs hanging on the walls and photos of the two of them together, smiling, laughing, holding hands . None of this seemed real. His clothes were still hanging in the closet, his books were in the bookcases. There were even a few old surfboards in the basement downstairs. It was as if nothing had ever happened, as if time stood still.

She thought of the family they'd been eager to start . She would never bear his children now. She would never have that part of him.

"He's everywhere," she said to Ann. "Just look around."

"Little by little, you'll have to begin to clear his things out," Ann replied.

That shocked Cindy. "Never," she breathed. "I'll never throw him away."

"No one's saying you're throwing him away. But little by little you'll need to take his things down, clear out the closets."

Suddenly Cindy wanted Ann to be gone. She couldn't even begin to imagine the pain Cindy was going through. If she could, she never would speak like this.

"Look, I know it's a terrible thing that happened," Ann said, "I know you're still in shock. These awful accidents happen, though. They're no one's fault."

Cindy felt her blood turn cold. "Accident?"

Ann stared at her. "Of course. It was an accident."

"Says who?" Cindy said.

"What are you talking about? The police in Barbados declared it an accident. Clint fell off the surfboard, it hit him on the head and snapped his neck."

"No," Cindy replied, "it didn't happen like that."

Ann's face turned pale. "Yes it did. The bruises on his body are consistent with the report. A sudden riptide came in."

"There was no riptide that afternoon. The sun was shining. It was a beautiful day."

"Cindy," Ann spoke slowly, "Riptides come suddenly and then they're gone."

"It was NOT an accident," Cindy intoned.

Ann stared back, shocked.

"According to who?" Ann said.

"Whose side are you on, Ann?" Cindy said, angry.

"Whose side? What are you talking about?"

"The police just wanted the case closed in the blink of an eye," Cindy said methodically.

Ann got up from her chair and started walking back and forth slowly. Cindy could tell how agitated her sister felt.

Cindy got up, too, and started pacing beside her sister. "Clint was a top tier surfer," Cindy continued. "He knew the ocean, he knew the waves. He'd surfed in much rougher waters. There was no reason for him to die."

Ann stopped and looked Cindy straight in the eye.

"Look," she said, "I know how tough this is for you. Don't make it worse than it is. Don't start imagining all kinds of things."

"I'm not imagining anything," Cindy said. "I've had plenty of time to think things over and nothing's gelling for me. It doesn't make sense."

Ann began rubbing her hands up and down her sides. It was an old habit of hers. She did it when she was nervous and didn't know what else to do.

"Cindy, I beg you, don't go crazy," she finally said. "I love you and I need you to be okay for me too."

Cindy's eyes filled with tears. "I'll never be okay," she said, "and I'm not going crazy. It's something I just *know.*"

"Let's leave it at that for now," Ann said softly. "It's common to think all kinds of things when someone you love suddenly dies. Your problem is that you've been cooped up in here for days. You're not thinking clearly. You're not changing, not showering, not even going outside."

"I don't want to," Cindy snapped back. "Let me be."

"There are more people who want to come visit. You need to let them in. You need to see them."

"I'm not ready!" Cindy yelled back.

"Well, there are some visitors that you have no choice about."

Cindy looked at her coldly. "Who?" she finally asked.

"Clint's family. They called. They're coming over today, at 3 o'clock."

"I'm not ready to see them," Cindy said.

"They didn't ask," Ann said.

Cindy's body clenched.

"Don't worry," Ann said, "They have to come. It's a duty call. But I won't let anything happen. I'll be here. It will all be fine."

If Cindy knew anything about Clint's family, she knew that a visit from them, even in the best of times, would be anything but fine.

Chapter 4

Cindy dreaded seeing Clint's family, but knew she had no choice. It's a duty call, she kept reminding herself. We're all in the same boat here.

Clint's family had objected to Cindy from the first day he brought her home. She wasn't tall enough, smart enough, rich enough for them. She wasn't slim enough either. His mother told him that Cindy's body would go to fat after they had a child and probably never recover. Cindy didn't come from their area either, as she was raised in Wisconsin. Nothing was good enough for them.

Cindy realized that Clint's mother would find anything she could to break up the relationship. But not only her—for any woman. His mother did all she could to cast every possible doubt. Clint had had two other long-term relationships before her, and Clint had told her that his mother had managed to poison them both.

Cindy had talked to Clint a lot about this . How could they buy this house only a mile away from his family? What would happen after they were married? How would his parents react when they had kids?

But he couldn't really see any problem, and he made all kinds of excuses for his mother, and told Cindy not to look for the worst . His sister Marge was a different story. Clint's relationship with Marge had always been rocky, although Marge and her mother were inseparable. Marge lived a few blocks away from her, and Marge couldn't stand to see Clint and his mother so close .

Marge got married a year ago. The man she married, Ralph—dark, quiet and inscrutable— was a lawyer, from a poor family on the other side of town. He'd put himself through college and law school and was doing well now - well enough to be accepted by the family . But they had always hoped Marge would marry James Torton, a rich kid from the neighborhood. Marge would have married him, too, but he left her suddenly, for someone else. Marge said she would carry the scars from that the rest of her life.

Now Cindy was getting ready for their visit. She knew she should put on something nicer. But she just couldn't bear to change. With Clint dead, she didn't feel entitled to wear anything nice. She would just have to greet his family in the lounging pants she'd been wearing, with the same old sweat shirt. She knew that as soon as they came in they would look her over from head to toe, watch her every move. They would scoff at her clothing. And if something were out of order, they'd be talking about it for days. But she didn't really care.

The family would also check the house to see that everything was exactly where it belonged. They were furious when Clint bought this place without consulting them . They said it didn't suit him and was too far away, down this long, deserted road. Who in their right mind would buy a clapboard, starter house that looked like a beach home?

Clint didn't seem to care what they thought of it, and just put his photos everywhere, even the ones they didn't like. Cindy's memorabilia were perched in full display on the white, wooden shelves—hand-painted porcelain ducks and birds. Clint's mother didn't like them either. What grown woman would display objects like that? And who had designed the living room decor? The couch had tropical, colored cushions on it, and there were plants that were much too large growing everywhere. It was clearly Cindy's influence, her lack of taste. This was definitely not the life she'd envisioned for her son. His mother had no compunction about telling him so, either . How Cindy landed someone like Clint baffled her mind.

Cindy was uneasy at the thought of seeing the family now. She knew they were devastated and had no idea how to comfort them. Thank

God Ann was still here. She would not have been able to face them alone. .

Ann was in the kitchen now preparing coffee and cake. Cindy scanned the living room quickly to make sure everything was in order. But no matter how much she tried to spruce it up, the room looked sad and tousled.

Cindy puffed the cushions on the sofa, and arranged them neatly. She had stacked the piles of gifts they'd received for the wedding in the corner. She'd forgotten all about them, hadn't noticed the gifts since she'd returned. They stood there as an awful reminder of a life that could have been.

Now she quickly went over, lifted them a few at a time, and brought them into Clint's study in the rear of the house. The last thing she wanted was to have the family looking the gifts over, asking for them to be opened or pushing her to send thank you cards. She would when she was ready. It was all way too much right now.

"How are you doing?" Ann called in from the kitchen.

Cindy could smell the delicious fragrance of coffee and homemade cookies wafting into the living room.

Ann walked out of the kitchen and looked Cindy over. Ann was wearing a casual pair of slacks and an old familiar, blue sweater. Her light brown hair was brushed neatly down around her moon-shaped faced face. Ann was deeply at home with herself. Whatever she wore, she looked lovely, ready for whatever circumstance presented itself. Cindy envied that. She often felt awkward, and Clint's family intensified that. When they were around, she felt as if she never made the grade.

Ann looked her over in disapproval. "If you're not going to change, will you at least just brush your gorgeous, tasseled hair."

Cindy smiled. Ann always tried to make her feel beautiful . The doorbell rang, and Cindy and Ann looked at each other.

"Can you answer it?" Cindy asked.

Ann nodded, and headed for the door.

Cindy went to the bathroom, closed the door, and listened. The quiet, muted voices carried through. Cindy splashed cold water on her puffy cheeks, and took a deep breath.

Finally, she opened the door.

Clint's family was already seated. His mother sat beside Clint's father on the sofa. They sat at opposite ends and did not touch. His sister Marge sat next to her husband Ralph in the sand-colored chairs that faced the couch. Everyone was dressed in either navy blue or black. Ann sat facing the family on a thin wooden bench. It had a long paisley cushion on it. The room felt stultifying.

Ann quickly got up when Cindy entered and pulled over a comfortable chair for her. Cindy wondered how she would ever get along without Ann at her side. As she sat down, she felt every eye in the family boring through her . Marge started coughing and Clint's mother put her head in her hands. It was a terrible moment for them all. Cindy wanted to say, *I'm sorry, I'm sorry*. But the words wouldn't come.

"Would you like some coffee and cookies?" Ann asked, getting up to serve them.

"Not right now," Clint's father mumbled. He seemed much weaker and sounded distant and sad, as if this were all much more than he could bear.

"This is the worst possible thing that could happen for my father," Marge blurted out. "He has to be careful of his heart and it's been hurting terribly all week long. He's on extra medication now," and she looked at Cindy darkly, as though perhaps, she was to blame.

"I'm so sorry," Cindy said.

"We thought you would take good care of Clint," his mother lifted her head and stared at Cindy. There was not an ounce of sympathy in her. The entire family was wrapped only in their own grief. "We still can't understand how something like this could have happened," his mother persisted.

Cindy felt her heart start to pound and her lips get dry. What were they intimating? Fortunately, Ann came to the rescue.

"This was a horrible accident," she said quietly. "If Cindy could have prevented it, she would have. She's suffering, too."

Ralph, Marge's husband, cleared his throat when Ann said that. "We're all suffering," he said. "We recognize that."

"Well, I'm glad to hear that," Ann replied.

"We didn't come here to argue," Ralph stated, in his flat, orderly, dry tone.

What did you come here for? Cindy wanted to ask them, but held her tongue. She could feel the raw emotion not only in her, but everyone there. It could explode at any moment and wreak havoc in their lives. She had heard of things like that happening after a death— families fighting, wild accusations, even when the death was expected, even when it was natural. Cindy placed her hands on her lap and folded them together.

"None of us are clear about what exactly happened," Ralph took the lead. It sounded as though he'd prepared his words to the letter.

In a swift moment, Cindy realized this was not a condolence call. The family wanted facts, information—they wanted someone to blame for this nightmare. Thankfully, Ann had some experience with these kinds of situations. Before she started her own consulting business, she was trained as a social worker and had worked in a hospital for a few years before her marriage .

Cindy looked at Ann, pleadingly. *Do something,* she wanted to say, *fill the empty spaces, answer their questions, make all this go away.*

Ann got the message.

"What would you like to know, Ralph?" she said.

"It's not just me, of course, it's the entire family," Ralph answered carefully.

"Of course," Ann replied professionally. "What questions can I answer for you?"

"I don't want to hear from *you,*" Clint's mother's face flushed. "It's Cindy I want to hear from. She's the one who was there."

"Cindy has already told everyone what happened," Ann said.

"No she hasn't. Not enough. I want to know more—much more."

"I know how hard this is for you," Ann said to Clint's mother quietly.

"No, you don't," his mother hissed. "Nobody can know what it's like for a mother to lose a son. Certainly not a new bride, who only knew him for a year. I knew him his whole life long. From the day he was born. I carried him inside me for nine months."

Cindy felt woozy again, almost like fainting. "I'm so sorry," she said to his mother.

His mother's head flipped upwards, like a cat. "Sorry isn't enough," she said.

Ann got up and stood between Cindy and her. "Excuse me," she interrupted, "but my sister is in pain as well. I hope you realize that."

"I don't realize anything," Clint's mother said. "I don't know how in the world I could have lost a son. And I want answers from the last person who saw him alive."

Cindy choked back the tears that were forming.

"We never felt good about this marriage," Marge chimed in. "There were a lot of questions which were unanswered."

"Like what?" Anne said.

Marge turned and looked to Ralph for help.

"Like why Clint, such a young man, would take out such a large insurance policy, just before a new marriage. It's not par for the course."

"I told Clint to tell you he was doing it," Cindy said. She had enough, and stood up. "I never wanted the policy. I told him not to, but he said he wanted to protect me, in case anything ever happened. Clint was like that. Very protective."

"You don't have to tell us who Clint was," Marge said.

"Then why do you have all these questions?" Cindy said.

"We've heard different stories about what happened on the island," Clint's father spoke up suddenly.

"From who?" Cindy asked.

"From different relatives."

"Your relatives weren't on the island," Cindy said forcefully.

"But everyone's looking into what happened," his father continued, "they all have different opinions."

Cindy felt ill. Clint's family was suspicious of everything, and she'd known it before they married. Even Ann warned her about it, but she hadn't paid a bit of attention . Now, for a quick moment, she was sorry . She didn't want to ever have to see any of them again.

Marge stood up suddenly and smoothed her black rayon dress. "For starters," she bristled, "you could tell us why in the world you chose to go to the East Coast of the island instead of the West? Everyone knows it's dangerous."

"We went for the surfing," Cindy answered quickly. "Some friends of Clint's recommended the place. I don't have to tell you that Clint loved to surf."

"He surfed his whole life and nothing happened," Marge repeated bitterly.

"He surfed rougher places, and was a fantastic swimmer. He was a lifeguard for years. He knew the ocean inside and out."

Cindy saw Clint's father's head bob up and down. She didn't know if he was sobbing or if he'd fallen asleep. No one else seemed to notice. Marge did, though.

"You see how sick dad is?" she said. "And all this has made it worse."

"I'm very sorry," Cindy said again.

Now his mother stood up and walked right up to where Cindy was sitting.

"When was the last time you saw my son alive? What was the last thing you said to each other?" Her eyes were squinting as if a strong light shone on them.

Cindy tried to remind herself to say calm, that his family were all in horrible pain.

She shouldn't take any of this personally. It was awful, though, to be forced to go back over that afternoon. But she wanted to give them whatever comfort she could.

"I last saw him in the afternoon. We were planning to go surfing together. It was about an hour or so after lunch. We went up to the room to change and I

suddenly began to have bad cramps. I got very tired. So, I lay down for a little nap instead. I planned to nap for about an hour and then go down and meet him on the beach."

"And?" his mother was relentless.

"And I overslept. I woke three hours later."

"That doesn't make sense," his mother said. "You suddenly had cramps from out of nowhere?"

"That's what happened," Cindy replied. "I jumped up, got out of bed and ran down to the beach to join him. He wasn't there."

"Where was he?" Ralph questioned.

"He wasn't there," Cindy repeated.

"Where do you think he was?" said Marge . "He was dead in the ocean." She turned on Ralph, who flinched.

"The hour of death," Ralph continued blankly, "was determined to be around five in the afternoon."

A long, dark pall hung over the room.

"Where is all of this going?" Ann interrupted.

"When did Cindy get down to the beach?" Ralph asked.

"I got down at about 5:15 or so," Cindy said.

"None of it makes sense." his mother started ringing her hands again. "He died a few minutes before you arrived? How is it possible?"

"When I got down there the beach was empty," Cindy repeated breathlessly. "I ran up and down. I couldn't find him."

"Were the two of you fighting? Was he sorry you ever got married?" The words poured out of Marge fitfully.

"That's enough," Ann said forcefully, and stood in front of Cindy to protect her from the onslaught. "This visit is over. I don't know what you're thinking, but you're way out of line."

"Why else wouldn't a bride go down to the beach with her husband when he's surfing? Why else would she suddenly have cramps and sleep all afternoon?"

Marge was on a rampage.

"What are you intimating?" Ann asked.

"The facts lead to questions," Ralph stood up. "We have to ask them. In honor of Clint's memory, we have to know what really went on."

Cindy felt herself choking. Was this horrible family accusing her of wrongdoing? From the start they wanted to disrupt the relationship - and even now, after his death?

"There were no witnesses to anything," Ralph continued. "No one knew you were asleep in your room?"

"The man who ran the hotel, Alex, saw me leave when I ran out to the beach," Cindy said.

"How convenient," Marge replied.

"I beg your pardon," Ann glared at her.

Cindy could barely hold her tongue. "I've thought about it myself," Cindy continued. "Who's really responsible? There are loopholes here, serious loopholes." She stared right back at Ralph. "Don't think I haven't wondered exactly what happened myself."

Ralph didn't so much as blink an eye. Again a strange, dark silence descended over them all. Cindy suddenly looked over at the wall and saw the photograph of her and Clint, smiling together, arm in arm, leaning against their new, small boat they had docked here in the cove. They had been so happy in every way. How could anyone think otherwise? Could Clint see what was going on now? What would it take to make him realize? Wasn't there something he could do to protect her now?

Cindy wished she had better answers to the questions they'd asked. She flashed back to the hotel room, to the moment she woke up that afternoon. She'd been disoriented. It was not like her to nap that long in the afternoon. And she didn't usually have cramps. She and Clint had been together every minute of the honeymoon. She'd had no intention of abandoning him. That was the last thing in her heart or mind.

She was not going to share these facts with the family, though, or defend herself in any way. It would only make things worse. Clearly, they hated her and wanted to punish her for everything. They were looking for any detail that could pin her up against the wall.

Once again Ann interrupted the tense situation.

"I think this is enough for now," she said. "Cindy looks exhausted and so does Clint's father. "

"When?" his mother suddenly burst out, standing. "When will I know the truth!?"

Chapter 5

After they left, both Cindy and Ann breathed a sigh of relief at exactly the same moment.

"How could someone so wonderful have a family like that?" Cindy said, trembling.

"Sit down, I'll bring you some tea," Ann said.

Cindy couldn't bring herself to sit on the sofa right where his parents had been sitting . "They're terrifying," she murmured.

"His family's struggling with a terrible loss," Ann said quietly.

"They're blaming me," Cindy felt her face grow red.

"Yes, they are," Ann said without flinching, "Cindy, I really think you should come home."

For a moment Cindy couldn't understand what Ann was saying. "I am home," she said.

"I mean, back to Wisconsin. You could move in with mother for awhile and I would be close by. I can't stay here forever. Frank is being a darling, but he also needs me. Sooner or later, he's going to tell me to come back."

Cindy's heart dropped at the thought of Ann leaving. In the back of her mind she knew this would be coming. Ann couldn't stay here forever. She'd been here way longer already than she should have. Tears filled Cindy's eyes.

"I can't go back and live with mother," Cindy said, forlorn. "It wouldn't work, she wouldn't be comfortable and neither would I. She needs her space."

"Well, you can get your own apartment near us. For a year or so anyway. It will help you get back to yourself again. Most of your friends are back home, too. You've only been East for a year and a half."

"This is my home now. And Clint's."

"He's not here anymore."

"But we bought it together. We picked it out, moved in, put the pictures on the walls. We started to plant the garden together. Clint's things are all over. How can I just leave everything behind?"

Ann took Cindy's hands. "Cindy, sweetheart," she said softly, "Clint's things are here. But he is not."

The words didn't sink in. Cindy couldn't grasp them. Looking around, she felt as though he were everywhere.

"You need to be close to people who love you, who will take care of you for awhile. You've been through a tremendous ordeal," Ann said.

"I have some new friends here," Cindy said. She thought of a few friends from work that she had lunched with, and others she'd met at the local book club. Her life here was beginning to grow roots. Most of the time, of course, Cindy had spent with Clint.

"I mean, you need to be near family," Ann said.

Cindy sat down on the sofa. Ann was more than a sister to her—she was a best friend. She wanted to go back and be close to her, but she also knew she couldn't. This was her home and she couldn't run from it. There was too much unfinished business, too many strands to be unraveled. She had wedding gifts to unpack and return. Thank you cards to write, letters to be answered. She had all of Clint's clothing and possessions to look after. And she had a job she loved as a research assistant at a top newspaper in the city. Cindy always loved to find little known facts, investigate details in a story. And her boss said she could take as much time as she needed; whenever she was ready, the job was waiting for her. Little by little, she'd get ready. She'd learn how to stand on her own two feet and make sense of all that had gone on.

"What about Clint's family?" Ann continued. "They're strange. They're dangerous. And they only live a mile away. I'm nervous leaving you here so close by."

"They don't have the key to the house," Cindy said swiftly, a wave of anger rising.

"This is my home, and Clint was *my* husband, whether they liked it or not. I'm sorry, Ann, really I am, but there's no way I can leave my home with Clint behind."

Cindy stormed away into her room and threw herself down on the bed. *This can't be happening,* she said to herself, over and over. Then she closed her eyes and pictured Clint, as if to bring him back to her. She remembered the two of them together at the wedding, kissing, holding hands, how beautiful everything had been. That is, until it came time for the speeches.

When it was Clint's mother's turn to say a few words, she stood up and spoke about Clint as a little boy, how wonderful he'd been then, and that she had no idea what happened when he grew up. Everyone had laughed, except Cindy. His mother said a few more words about Clint, the ladies' man, then fluffed her hair and sat down. She didn't say a word about Cindy. When it was Marge's turn, she went on and on about what a wonderful catch Clint was. Again not a word about Cindy, or welcoming her into the family. Cindy'd had a sinking feeling right then, but just let it drift away . She wasn't going to let them ruin her wedding. Soon she and Clint would be away from them all, the two of them alone together, on their honeymoon . He was hers now, and the family could never take him away. Or so she imagined.

Cindy's mind drifted back again to the honeymoon. They'd both been so thrilled to be in Barbados, it seemed that everything there was welcoming them, the sky, sand, rolling waves . They'd laughed and joked about everything, explored all kinds of nooks and crannies, saw the flying fish, whistling turtles, coral reefs, chatted with locals and guests at the hotel. It was as if they were exactly where they belonged and nothing bad could ever happen to them. She remembered snorkeling with Clint in the warm, turquoise water, swimming among gorgeous, slippery, red, green and yellow fish. As they swam, their legs intertwined, it seemed as if they would never be apart.

"We were put on this earth just for each other," Clint had whispered to her late one night as they danced at the hotel.

Cindy felt that way, too. She didn't know what she had done to deserve this kind of happiness.

Now she began to go over and over each moment, looking for the reason why everything had gone so wrong. She felt helpless not knowing, as if she were just letting the ocean sweep Clint away. How could it? He was such a good person, had always reached out to help everybody. Why would this terrible thing happen to him? It didn't make any sense. There had to be an explanation. Maybe someone wanted to murder him . She had to find out who.

She went over each day before the wedding carefully, again and again. Clint had been more stressed than usual the last few weeks leading up to the marriage. She hadn't thought much of it then, knew it was normal for tensions to build before the big day. His family only added to the tension, had something to complain about every day. They were upset with everything about the wedding—the seating, the flowers, the band. There was nothing that felt right to them. And they blamed Cindy for all of it. Clint's mother even had Ralph call and ask Clint if he really knew the woman he was marrying. After all, they'd only been together for a year.

"Why do they hate me so much?" Cindy'd asked frequently.

Clint refused to consider that question.

"My parents don't hate anyone. They love you like I do. They're just nervous about me."

Cindy didn't get it. She wondered more deeply now about the extent of their hatred. What kind of action might it have led them to take? Were there secrets she had no idea about? Had he been holding something back from her? And, now that he was gone, would she ever know?

She broke down sobbing. *It's not fair, it's not fair*, she murmured, *he didn't deserve it*. Not Clint. And, with tears uncontrollably pouring down her face, she fell into a torn, fitful sleep. In which followed, day after day, night after night, a parade of restless nightmares.

Chapter 6

3 weeks later

Even though it was half past ten o'clock in the morning, Cindy was still sleeping . Oblivious to the world around her, she dreamt that it was early winter, the first snow falling, and that Clint was back. They were together, shoveling, making a path up to their home. They had on big fur hats and puffy gloves. Clint's face was red, brushed by the cold wind. He said that after they finished shoveling, they could build a snowman in front of the house. Cindy was excited. She hadn't built a snowman for years, and she'd find a funny hat to put on him, like the one Clint wore.

Laughing, they built a huge, fat snowman, with red buttons in his eyes.

But as soon as Cindy put its hat on, the snowman began to melt.

"It's melting," she yelled to Clint, who suddenly couldn't hear her.

Desperate, she started to scoop up the melting snow, but then awoke abruptly .

Ann was in her bedroom, pulling open the curtains, letting in the light of day .

"It's morning, wake up," Ann said.

The light was too bright. Cindy threw her arm over her eyes. "Not yet. Close the curtains."

"Time to get up," Ann was moving briskly around the room, going from window to window. "Come on, it's getting late. Visitors are coming. Today's the day."

"I'm not up to it, " Cindy mumbled.

"You have no choice," Ann's voice rose higher. "You told a lot of people they could come today. They want to see you. It's time, Cindy. It's three weeks now."

Cindy rubbed her eyes and slowly stretched. "I don't know," she said.

"There's nothing to know," Ann said. "Just get up, shower and change."

Cindy pulled off the covers and dragged herself out of bed.

The weather had grown warmer as the end of May approached. Ann had opened all the windows in the house, letting the spring breezes in. The forsythia were in full array and the trees in the yard outside were bursting into bloom .

As Cindy splashed water over her face in the bathroom, she thought of how much Clint loved the springtime. They'd loved waiting for the weather to get warm together, watching the earth come back to life. At her urging, he had even helped plant a garden in the back before they left for their honeymoon. Cindy didn't know if she could ever go back there and care for the young sprouts that must be shooting up.

Cindy could smell Ann baking brownies in the kitchen. Time had a way of moving forward, even if she did not want it to. She knew she couldn't go on like this forever. There was a stream of people waiting to visit and offer condolences. Clint had been raised in Cove Bay since he was a boy and the entire community wanted to come and bring food and offers of help. Some, of course, wanted to come out of curiosity, to see Clint's new home and wife. They might have seen Cindy in passing, but she had not been a regular here in town. There were rumors all around town that Clint's family wasn't happy with Cindy. No one knew exactly why.

Cindy had to screen the visitors carefully. Of course Clint's old friends had to be welcomed. She also had to receive visits from people at the company he'd worked for - DGB Oil. Ann told her that the company had been calling daily, asking after Cindy, especially Henry Greerson, Clint's boss. Clint had been a rising star in the company. Clint was smart, assertive, outspoken and did a thorough job with everything. Working as he did, researching the effects of offshore drilling on the environment, he was an important voice. And speaking at many conferences, meetings and lunches, he was in the public eye. He'd even recently been sent to Washington to speak both to members of congress and significant lobbies in the oil industry.

Clint had loved what he did and all that went with it. It was as if he were on a personal crusade to create a crucial balance - care for the wildlife and environment and find a way for much needed drilling to be done safely and wisely. Clint wasn't someone who could be easily replaced. Not by anyone .

In preparation for receiving visitors, Cindy went to her closet and looked over her clothing. She usually dressed simply, in slacks, jeans, short skirts and shirts. There wasn't much in her closet to cover the days of visitors she now had to receive. She wanted to make a good impression. This was Clint's memory she was taking care of. They would remember him, partially, through the wife he had chosen, and she was determined to play the role well.

"Hurry up and get dressed. It's almost time," Ann called from the other room.

Cindy went into the bedroom and slipped into a simple, dark-green, linen dress in which she always felt at ease. It had a little scoop neck, medium sleeves, a lovely bodice and fell below her knees gracefully. Then she slipped into gray and green open sandals, went into the bathroom and brushed her long, auburn, tousled hair. Without a doubt, her hair was the most striking part of her, she thought, combined with the light freckles on her forehead. Clint always loved it when she brushed her hair. He would stand in the doorway and watch her for hours.

"You have no idea how beautiful you are," he'd always say. "All the guys are crazy jealous of me. They don't know how I landed someone like you." Then he'd come over and kiss her on the neck. As the months went by, she'd begun to believe him.

Now she didn't know who she was anymore.

Cindy brushed her hair for a long time, not really looking in the mirror much. It was hard to see herself standing there, getting dressed, without Clint nearby. What was the point of it?

The doorbell rang.

Oh no, she thought, *they're here.*

At least the family wouldn't be coming today. That was something to be grateful for.

She stayed in the bathroom a moment longer, and leaned against the door, listening to Ann let the visitors in. The voices rose and fell, then there was quiet. She couldn't hide here forever.

She straightened her shoulders and walked out into the living room, as if it were a normal visit, as if nothing horrifying had happened to turn all their lives upside down. *Clint always wanted me to be brave*, she thought, as she sailed in. No one smiled as she entered.

Clint's friends had arrived, as well as some acquaintances of Cindy's from work.

"I can't even imagine what you must be going through," Tina, a friend of Clint's said.

"Unbearable," another friend, Barbara, chimed in.

Cindy was grateful for their kindness.

"Clint told us how much he loved you," Tina said, leaning forward. "He felt like such a lucky man."

Cindy choked up. "Thank you," she managed. "I was the lucky one."

"We live just a few miles away," Tina offered. "We're here if you need us."

Cindy felt grateful. "That's so kind," she said and meant it.

The doorbell rang again. Al, a longtime pal of Clint's walked in, carrying a gift basket. He'd been the best man at the wedding. "Listen Cindy," he said right away. "I was Clint's best man and still am. You need anything, you let me know. That's what a best man is for."

He put the basket on the coffee table, started unwrapping it and giving some fruit, crackers and pieces of candy to all of them. Cindy noticed that Ann seemed to feel calmer as the afternoon went on. There were people nearby to support Cindy. She wouldn't be totally alone.

They all remembered Clint, what a good friend he was, how much fun he was to be with, what amazing things he could have done with his life.

"The damn guy always walked a thin line though," Al suddenly said, "Things would be going great in his life and then he'd always turn around and spend some time on the wild side."

"What do you mean?" Cindy asked, startled.

"Danger, he had a taste for it. Nothing terrible, just some adventures he couldn't pass by. For a while it was car racing."

Cindy hadn't heard anything about this.

"Yeah," Al continued, "like when his car crashed in the third race he entered."

"It was terrifying," Tina said.

"His mother really freaked on him, even though he walked out of the wreck without a scratch. The crowd let out a scream when they saw him alive. But he gave up racing anyway. He was always lucky in strange kinds of ways."

"I guess his luck ran out," Tina said, sadly.

"Jesus," Al said. "I just can't believe this. How did it happen?"

The doorbell rang again. Ann got up and let Henry Greerson in.

Clearly, Greerson had come straight from work. He still wore a pin striped suit and tie and had the paper rolled under his arm. Probably read it on the train ride out. Cindy hadn't expected him to come. He walked in, stopped for a moment, and gave Cindy a long look.

"How are you doing, Cindy?" he said.

"Thank you for coming," Cindy replied.

"Of course," he said. "I would have come sooner. Your sister said you weren't taking visitors."

"I couldn't in the beginning."

"Naturally."

There was something off-putting about him. He had thin lips, hazel, piercing eyes and a sallow complexion, even though the days were warm and sun plentiful. She supposed he lived in the city and didn't get much time outdoors.

"I want you to know that I represent everyone in the company when we tell you how sorry we are. Clint is a great loss. If there is anything we can do to help your transition, you must feel free to call on us."

Cindy shivered. She did not feel she could call on this man for anything. As he sat down and made himself comfortable, she vaguely remembered that he had flown out to Barbados right after Clint's death. He had been the other one to identify the body. She also remembered that Clint had spoken well of him.

Cindy saw Al looking at him carefully, too. Greerson seemed out of synch with the group that had gathered—too formal, smug, a bit intimidating.

Ann stood up. "Would you care for a cup of coffee, Mr. Greerson?" she asked.

"That would be lovely," he replied.

Ann left to get the coffee and pastries and he turned to Cindy. "You have quite a wonderful sister," he said.

"Yes," she said softly, wondering how he knew Ann was her sister. "More than wonderful. In fact, I couldn't have gotten along at all without her these past days."

"How long is she staying?" Barbara piped up.

"Forever," Cindy laughed.

Greerson looked surprised. "She's moving here to be with you?"

Cindy was taken aback. How did he know Ann didn't live nearby?

"Who knows," Cindy replied jokingly. "Right now it feels like anything could happen. The world seems upside down."

"Hell, this world *is* upside down," Al said. "When a great guy like Clint is washed away, what can you count on anymore?"

"Terrible accidents make you feel that way," Greerson agreed.

"I'm not so sure it was an accident," Cindy suddenly said.

Greerson flinched, and so did the others.

"That's a weird thing to say," Al looked at her strangely.

"The more I think about it, the less sure I am about how Clint died," Cindy spoke naturally, the words just pouring out. "It doesn't add up. There are plenty of other things that could have happened."

"Like what?" Greerson said.

You could have heard a pin drop. Everyone listened to Cindy intently. Ann walked back in the room with coffee, and stopped.

"I went online and looked up some facts," Cindy continued. "There are assaults and murders on the Eastern Coast of Barbados regularly. There's one case after another. The police are used to them. It's part of the routine. Nothing much is done."

Ann interrupted. She didn't want Cindy to go on like this in front of others. "It's easy to imagine all kinds of things when someone you love has suddenly died," she said, to ease the tension that was building.

"I'm not imagining anything," Cindy said, "I'm doing research."

"Research on what?" Greerson pressed her.

"Cindy is a research assistant at a newspaper," Anne said. "It comforts her to check all kinds of facts. Even when she was little, she enjoyed doing that. I remember her going through magazine after magazine, trying to find out this or that." She smiled again, trying to lighten the atmosphere, but it did not lift.

"That's a dangerous path to take," Greerson said quickly. "Suspecting Clint's death was a murder. Thinking like that can create a lot of distress, for you and everyone."

"I totally agree," Ann said.

Thankfully, the doorbell rang again.

"Now I see why you're staying here for such a long time," Greerson said to Ann. "You need to take care of your sister until she calms down and sees things clearly."

Cindy detested this man on the spot. Who was he to come here and suggest she wasn't seeing things clearly? What was it to him? What made him think *he* saw everything so clearly?

Ann went to the door and to everyone's surprise, Tom Mallord, the pastor who had both married them and done the funeral service, came in. He and Clint had had a close relationship for many years. Clint thought the world of him. Mallord carried a little package, neatly wrapped in his hand.

"Hello, Cindy," he said as he walked in, and handed her the package. "This is for you. It's something I hope will help you through the days ahead."

"Thank you so much," Cindy replied, taking the package. She hardly knew him, but always enjoyed the time they'd had together.

Ann pulled out a chair for him and he sat down. Then she introduced Mallord to Greerson. He knew all the other guests in the room.

"You came at the perfect moment," Greerson said. "We were just talking about the best way to view what happened to Clint."

Mallord raised his eyebrows. "A big question," he said.

Greerson looked at Cindy, as if expecting her to once again voice her fears . She said nothing.

"Cindy was just saying she's not sure that Clint's death was an accident."

Once again the room grew steely quiet. Mallord listened intently without changing his expression.

"She's been researching murders on the East Coast of Barbados," Greerson went on derisively.

Cindy noticed Mallord looking at her thoughtfully.

"Sometimes the best thing," Greerson went on, "is to see a therapist to clear your mind and bring you back to reality."

Cindy felt little drops of perspiration forming over her forehead and chin. He was suggesting she go to therapy because she thought Clint's death might not have been an accident? . Didn't she have a right to put the pieces of the puzzle together in a way that made sense to her? Did that mean she was crazy?

She wondered what Mallord thought. He had a wonderful reputation, lived simply with his wife in a small house the parish provided, and spent long hours with his congregation.

"Do you agree with him?" Cindy asked Mallord pointedly.

He didn't answer off the cuff, but paused, and finally said, "Therapy can be good when needed. So can prayer and contemplation. And time always has a way of showing us what has truly gone on."

Cindy now saw why Clint had liked Tom so much.

"Just the way the ocean brings everything up to shore," he continued, "the truth cannot help but be brought to light."

Greerson had enough. He got up and brushed off his suit.

"Well, thanks for the sermon," he said laughingly, "but I have a long trip back to the city tonight. There's a lot of unfinished business to take care of. We have plenty to do to deal with Clint's loss."

Cindy felt oppressed by his presence in the room and was tremendously relieved that he was leaving . "Thank you for coming," she said politely.

"It's my pleasure," he answered, looking directly at her. "And, as I said, don't let stray thoughts drive you crazy. You are not alone with this. I'll certainly be around."

When he left it felt as if a dark cloud had lifted and the evening light could shine in.

*

Later that night, in bed, her head swimming, Cindy noticed the little package Tom Mallord gave her, sitting on the end table. It was beautifully wrapped, in gold paper. She reached over and opened it slowly.

Inside was a small Bible. Touched to the core, Cindy cradled it in her hands, remembering the wonderful funeral service Tom Mallord had conducted for Clint. The pews at the funeral service were filled to the brim, and a haunted silence filled the place. Tom Mallord spoke simply, saying no one could fathom the ultimate will of God, or really understand how something like this could happen. But we all could reach out to one another and offer kindness and solace. That much was in our grasp. Cindy'd felt comforted by his honesty.

Some of Clint's friends got up and spoke about what a wonderful person he'd been and how they couldn't imagine life without him. Cindy shivered the entire time and could not say a word. Neither could Clint's mother, who sat in the front in a black, silk suit, staring ahead, in subdued rage.

Clint's sister Marge, dressed in dark blue silk, pearl earrings and a pearl necklace, spoke in measured tones. Cindy didn't believe a word she said and the sound of her voice grated at her. Clint's father sat doubled over for most of the service. When he got up at the end of the ceremony to shake hands, he couldn't seem to remember anyone's name.

Cindy looked down at the Bible, opened it up and ruffled through the pages. Could it possibly hold some answers for her? Could anything really give her solace in a time like this?

She opened the book randomly, and it opened on Psalm 84. She read it slowly. *Those who pass through the Valley of Thorns, they transform it into a wellspring. With blessings the rain will cloak it. They advance from strength to strength.*

The Valley of Thorns, she thought. Yes, that was what this was. But she didn't see how she would ever get out of it.

*

Greerson was standing there in a gray raincoat, carrying a black umbrella, laughing uncontrollably. She ran up to him to tell him to open the umbrella, that it was going to start pouring. He just kept laughing and paid no attention. She grabbed the umbrella from him, yanked her hardest to get it open. He pulled it back, enraged. Before long the two of them were in a full out tug of war.

She woke swiftly and sat up in bed. She shook her head several times to wipe the dream away.

Cindy hadn't been able to stop thinking about Greerson. She resented his inferring that she wasn't seeing things clearly. Above all, she prized herself on her ability to ferret out the truth of any situation. She had worked long hours at her job, making sure no important detail was missing in the research she did. It hadn't been easy landing a job at one of the best papers in New York City. Even though it was an entry level position, they soon gave Cindy more and more responsibility, with bigger and bigger articles. It was up to her to check the significant facts, dig deeper into the backgrounds of the people mentioned in the piece. Cindy was a huge asset. It was common knowledge that she had a wonderful future ahead of her.

As she headed downstairs, she found Ann in the kitchen, over the stove, stirring a pot of oatmeal as she did every morning. Cindy sat at the kitchen table. It was covered with a red checked tablecloth and placed near the window, in the sun.

"I've got a theory I want to run by you, Ann," Cindy said.

Ann kept stirring. This was Cindy's third theory this week . She knew Ann didn't like it, but had to continue anyway.

"We can't rule out that someone in the family got Clint killed," Cindy started.

"Oh God," Ann breathed.

"They dwell on me, they blame me, but I'm just a convenient cover. When you think about it, there's a lot they get by making it seem like there's something wrong with me."

"Who made you the detective here?" Ann breathed out heavily. "Go back to work.

Research stories at the paper. Keep all your fact checking there."

"And, don't forget the insurance money," Cindy barely heard what Ann said . "If Clint is gone and it's my fault, the money will all go to them."

Ann stopped stirring the oatmeal, and spun around. "Think a minute about what you're saying, Cindy. Clint's own family, who love him, would have him killed for insurance money? Why? They have plenty of money on their own."

"Someone in the family could be pathologically jealous—"

Ann's voice grew shriller. "Enough to have him killed?"

"We have to consider every angle."

"No, you don't," Ann tossed the wooden spoon down on the table. "You sound as if you're losing your mind."

"I'm thinking things through."

"You're becoming obsessed, " Ann continued.

"Listen, time is passing. I can't stay here forever. You're making it harder and harder for me to go."

Cindy knew what a strain she'd been on Ann, and she felt badly about it. Ann always brought a sense of balance and normalcy to her days. Cindy felt safe around her. She'd been dreading the day when Ann would tell her that she had to go.

Ann's voice had a thin edge to it. "I can't go home with a peaceful heart with you thinking these terrible thoughts. You sound paranoid."

Ann turned back to the stove. The oatmeal was ready. She turned off the fire, poured the oatmeal into two earthenware bowls and put them on the table. Then she went to pour fresh coffee for both of them, in two hand-painted mugs. The mugs were engagement presents from Cindy's old friends, back in Wisconsin. For a moment, Cindy felt homesick.

"I don't mean to be a burden," she said.

"Forget it," Ann said. "Eat your breakfast."

Ann loved to prepare food, and Cindy loved home-cooked meals. It was something their mother never had any time for. She'd been too busy working and running around town with her friends, and boyfriends, after Cindy's dad died . Ann had taken on the role of mother in Cindy's life.

Cindy and Ann starting eating breakfast. Cindy hated defending herself, having to prove she was just like everyone else. She never wanted to be just like everyone else. She just wanted to be who she was.

"I'm NOT crazy."

"Listen, I think you need to reach a point, and I'm not saying it's today, where you are just going to have to accept what happened with Clint, and move on," Ann declared.

Cindy knew Ann had her best interests in mind, but her words hurt. She would never move on. How could she?

"I'm doing just fine," said Cindy.

"How?" Now Ann was annoyed. " You haven't been able to open one gift from the wedding. You haven't been able to write one thank you note. You refuse to consider leaving this place. Clint's mother and sister live one mile away - and they've been calling too much. Way too much."

Cindy's stomach dropped. "Really?"

"Sometimes they call three or four times a day. You'd know if you ever checked your cell. Now they're calling my cell, too. Not to mention the landline. "

Cindy's body clenched .

"They want to come here and grill you again, get fact after fact."

"They're turning everything around," said Cindy, "pointing the finger at me."

"I can't stay here and protect you from them forever. They're devastated and furious."

"That's what I mean," Cindy said.

"It doesn't mean they killed their son," Ann seemed as if she were on the verge of trembling. "It's natural to feel that way after such a horrible loss."

Cindy fell silent.

Ann came closer, put her hand on Cindy's arm. "Cindy, listen to me, I really think it's time for you to go back to work. It would be good for you. You loved your job and it would take your mind off Clint."

"I don't want to take my mind off Clint," Cindy shot back, alarmed . "I want to remember every little thing. Take good care of him."

"He's not here to take care of," Ann breathed.

"I can take good care of his memory, though."

"Okay," Ann relented, "You want to take care of Clint's memory? Fine. The best way to do that would be to sell the house, take his things with you, and get away from his family. Take money from the sale of the house and come back home for a while. That will buy you some time. You won't have to work for a while, you can unwind, go through all his things and make some kind of memorial."

Cindy wasn't having it. "There's no way I'm selling this house or leaving it behind."

Ann's face was getting red . Her voice got louder. "Okay, fine. In that case, clean this place up! Unpack the gifts!, Throw out the empty boxes, send thank you notes, remove the clutter. You haven't unpacked your luggage from your honeymoon for Christ's sake!"

"Please," Cindy said, holding her head in her hands. "I'm not ready."

"Well, the time has come! You have to be ready. Whether you want to or not," Ann said, over her limit. "You have to open your mail, answer phone calls, fill the fridge with food, set a time when you're going to go back to the office—start your life over again. You can't just lay around here, dreaming up theories on what might have happened to Clint."

Cindy put her hands over her ears. "I hear you," she yelled back.

Ann pulled Cindy's hands away. "*Really* hear me, Cindy," she yelled. "You're in limbo and it can't go on."

Ann's voice was shrill and painful.

"Do it for me," Ann suddenly looked tearful.

That stopped Cindy cold. Ann had done so much for her .

"All right," she said, softening, "I'll do it. I'll get started."

"Good," Ann said, relieved . "Because I've bought a plane ticket. I'm going home."

"Go home?" It was as though someone punched Cindy in the heart. "When?"

"The day after tomorrow," Ann said. "I have to, I have no choice."

"Oh God," Cindy ran to Ann and threw her arms around her, giving her a huge hug.

"It's okay, Ann, I understand."

Tears started falling down Cindy's face.

"You've been the most wonderful sister in the world, and I'll never forget all that you've done."

"You're a wonderful sister, too," Ann sounded teary. "And I can't bear the thought of losing you."

"You'll never lose me," Cindy was taken aback.

"Sometimes when one person dies, they take others with them," said Ann. "Some people never get over a loss. I just mean, I need you strong and healthy. Please."

Chapter 7

The next day Cindy let Ann borrow her car, and Ann left early in the morning to go into town and pick up a few things she needed to pack.

Now the house was completely silent, except for the sound of the rain. For the first time, Cindy was alone.

It felt odd. She paced the empty rooms, seeing reminders of her life with Clint everywhere, and finally, she realized that she couldn't go on like this. She had to do something, or else risk losing her mind.

It was a good time to start putting things in order, she thought. She put on jeans and an old tee shirt, and brought the boxes of gifts into the living room, piling them high . She made trip after trip, her arms full of packages, not realizing how many they'd received.

She got a pad and pencil to make a note of who to thank. It was strange to open the gifts alone, they were for a marriage that barely got started. A marriage that had lasted less than a week.

As she placed the boxes out on the living room floor, Cindy thought of the day they became engaged. It was only three months after they'd met. A regular weekday, they were going to meet after work at Central Park, go for a walk, and then grab a quick dinner. When Cindy saw Clint walking towards her, she knew something was different. He had a huge grin on his face. Clint wasn't one to hide his emotions, ever.

"We're going for a horse and buggy ride," he told her and practically picked her up and put her into the buggy."

Cindy had laughed. She loved his surprises. She loved everything about him.

So, when he'd asked her to marry him in the horse and buggy, it felt completely natural. She was ecstatic. There wasn't a doubt in her mind that he was the one. There wasn't a doubt in his mind either.

Cindy had looked at Clint and felt how grateful and fortunate she was. From almost the first moment she met him, she knew he was the man she wanted to live her life with. Tall, rugged, handsome and determined, he was the most honest and caring man she'd ever met. There were many new doors Clint had opened for her, and she'd walked through them gladly, always excited to find out about something new. He'd introduced her to new food, friends, ideas, activities and encouraged her in everything she did.

"You're a brave woman, Cindy," he once told her. "That's what I love most about you. "

That shocked her. She'd never thought of herself as brave. She just loved discovering new things and Clint had been a wonderful guide .

Now she sat down on the floor and opened the box closest to her. Inside was a large, crystal punch bowl . The card read: "Love and congratulations. To years and years of happiness. The Jennisens."

Cindy held the punch bowl in her arms. It was round and sparkling, full of happiness. There were so many wonderful occasions they could have used it for. She looked at it for another moment, then she put it back in the box, making a note who it was from. She would return it.

Next she opened a long, thin box. In it was a beautiful, ceramic vase. The card inside said, "May your new life be filled with beauty." Cindy stroked its smooth surface and envisioned the fresh flowers from the garden she and Clint could have filled it with.

A long wide, heavy box contained silverware. "Congratulations to a beautiful couple," signed from a friend of Cindy's mother.

She wrote the name and address of each person who sent the gift, then re-wrapped it in its box, to return. With each gift she returned, she felt their marriage slip further away.

As she opened packages, Cindy heard the phone ring. She let it ring. She couldn't stop every time someone called. And she didn't really feel like talking to anyone anyway.

There were linens, glasses, wall hangings, picture frames....

She'd opened and closed about seven gifts before something odd caught her eye: an eight by ten envelope, stuck between two boxes.

Cindy picked up the envelope and looked at it. It was addressed to Clint, postmarked six weeks ago, with no return address. Someone had sent it before the wedding. She didn't know how it landed here—probably misplaced in all the confusion.

What could it be?

She quickly opened it up and took out a piece of paper. A photo was inside of it. On the paper was scrawled - *For You* .

She held up the photo and saw a candid picture of a beautiful woman—tall, dark haired, walking down the street with a little child at her side.

Cindy held the photo closer, looked at it at different angles, turned it to the light. Her hands shook as she realized that the little boy looked startlingly like Clint.

She turned the photo over to see if there was a date. There wasn't. Her heart started beating faster.

Who was this woman, and when was the picture taken?

Who sent it? Why? Did Clint know her? Was something going on between them?

Cindy stared at it, trying to make sense of everything.

Her heart started to break, but she stopped it. She refused to jump to the worst conclusions. She knew that Clint had had girlfriends in the past. He'd told her those relationships were all over, didn't care about anyone but her anymore. No woman he knew was anything like her. She was the one he wanted .

She had to stay calm and keep a clear mind. She wasn't going to let one photo destroy her memory of Clint, or let him be smeared in any way. But she did have to find out more about it. For sure, something strange was happening. And this photo confirmed it. Had they sent other envelopes like this? Had Clint been hiding them?

Cindy decided to go into Clint's study to check it out further. She hadn't been able to spend time in it before . It was his private space, full of his belongings and memories. She felt like an intruder even at the thought of going in. But this photo jarred her. Someone had wanted him to have it before the wedding. She needed to know more.

Cindy got up and went straight into the study where Clint's computer, papers and files were stored. The room had a slanted, white wooden plank ceiling, smaller windows, and a knotty wooden floor, with a shaggy, navy throw rug. Clint had loved this room. The rug belonged to him since college. He'd taken it with him everywhere.

His files were stored in boxes along the back wall under the white wood bookshelves he had put up. There was a small desk in the corner, catty corner to the window with his computer, a little cactus plant, and all kinds of papers strewn on it. The window was open and you could smell the wisteria outside, wafting in. She could hear the light rain falling on the roof. It soothed Cindy.

This room was just for Clint. He loved having privacy and separate space, said it would keep the marriage strong. He always said that a good marriage always needed time together and time apart. Cindy had no problem with that. There was another small room, next to Clint's, that was going to be Cindy's study. She could sketch, make her collages, read, or do whatever she wanted in it. That room stood there empty, waiting to be filled . Cindy had no desire to go in it now. Clint's study was the place she had to be now, near him in any way she could.

It felt good to go in, sit down on the shag rug and breathe the damp, spring air. Cindy felt Clint's presence everywhere. She wanted to put the photo on Clint's desk, but it was messy. First she stuffed some of his papers in drawers and pushed others to the side. Then she sat down at the desk, put the photo in front of her and opened the computer.

This photo was a find. Clint had to have known the woman in it. She might have been one of his old girlfriends. The family probably knew her, for sure. Did they send the photo to remind Clint of her? Cindy wouldn't put it past them.

Cindy had to find out who the woman was. She didn't know where it would lead, but she was grateful at last, to have something specific to focus on .

She scanned the photo onto the computer, then logged into Facebook and used the face recognition software. The woman's name popped up - Heather Krane. Cindy went to her Facebook page to find out more.

The page was blocked. Private.

Distressed, Cindy thought a minute about what to do. She could Friend her, but she didn't know the woman, and doubted that she would accept. And besides, there wasn't enough time to wait and see. Cindy wanted to talk to her as soon as possible.

Then she had an idea . Heather Krane could be one of Clint's Facebook friends. He had hundreds and hundreds of them. Cindy could log back into Facebook as Clint and check his page.

Her hands trembled as she typed Clint's password to get in as him . His Facebook page quickly appeared. There he was, smiling out at the world, and there Cindy was, standing beside him, announcements of the wedding all over, messages of good wishes from friends. Cindy couldn't bear looking at any of it.

She quickly checked his friends and suddenly found her: Heather Kane.

Cindy took a quick, deep breath. She remembered once hearing that nothing could be hidden forever, every crime leaves a trace. Especially with computers, she thought. She was definitely onto something.

She clicked onto Heather's page and her picture appeared, along with her husband, friends and family. Cindy looked at all of them closely. Heather seemed to have a good life. She was married, lived in Philadelphia, had a lovely husband and little boy. Cindy looked at the little boy for a long time. It was strange to see him. He was beautiful, with strawberry blonde hair. And he looked just like Clint. Or was Cindy imagining things?

Whether her mind was playing tricks or not, she had to go forward . How did Clint know this woman? Had they remained in touch? Was it the family who sent him this photo? Or could it have been someone else? Heather, possibly? Did this beautiful child have anything to do with Clint?

Cindy quickly wrote down Heather's contact information, including her address. She wanted to talk to her.

Cindy looked at Heather's phone number. She could call immediately and introduce herself. But she had no idea how Heather would react to the call. Why would she talk to a complete stranger? And, if Heather had been following Clint's life, she might recognize that Cindy was Clint's wife and freeze up.

Cindy realized she'd have to go to Heather's home, in person, take her by surprise, meet up face to face.

She was actually staring at Heather's number, when her phone started ringing . Unsettled, Cindy grabbed it and immediately picked up. A male voice was on the other end. She didn't recognize it.

"Is this Mrs. Cindy Blaine?"

"Yes?" Cindy said. The voice sounded official.

"This is Officer Judd Lawson. I'm calling from North Alliance hospital. Are you the sister of Ann Blaine?"

Cindy's heart started pounding. Why would an officer be calling?

"What is it?" Cindy asked. "Is she OK?"

"Your sister has been in a car accident."

Cindy bolted upright.

"She's at North Alliance Hospital, in the emergency room. Please get there as soon as possible."

"What kind of accident?" Cindy gasped. "Is she OK?"

"Mam, you're going to need to get down here right away."

Chapter 8

Ann's eyes were closed when Cindy got to her side. She was tucked in a cubicle on a bed, in the emergency room, behind a green and white hanging curtain. Cindy pulled the curtain aside, slipped into the cubicle and sat down beside her. Ann's eyes fluttered open for a second and then shut again, as if drifting off to sleep.

Cindy grabbed her hand. "I'm here, Ann. I'm here. You're going to be just fine."

Ann seemed to smile, but didn't answer.

"They're going to take wonderful care of you."

Ann, eyes closed, didn't respond. Had she heard her?

A nurse pulled the curtains aside and came into the cubicle. She was a big, heavy, black woman, in her mid-fifties with short hair. Cindy was grateful to see her.

"Let's keep her awake," the nurse said to Cindy. "After they hit their head, it's good to keep them awake." Then she turned to Ann, "Hi there, honey," she shook her arm gently.

Cindy was relieved that the nurse was with them. "What happened?" she asked her, alarmed.

"Your sister's gonna be admitted for a full work up. We're waiting for a bed upstairs."

"How did this happen?" Cindy asked the nurse . Her mouth felt dry and her hands clammy.

"A police officer will be here to take information," the nurse continued. "It's routine."

Tears filled Cindy's eyes. She leaned towards her sister, "Are you okay, Ann?"

Ann opened her eyes slightly.

She moved her lips ever so slightly. She was trying to speak.

"What?" Cindy asked, leaning in close.

"Brakes…" Ann whispered.

Cindy stared at her, not understanding.

Ann reached over and grasped Cindy's wrist.

"No…brakes," Ann whispered, barely audible.

Then she closed her eyes again.

"Ann?" Cindy asked. "Ann?" she repeated, louder. "Are you saying that my car's brakes didn't work?"

But Ann was passed out.

Cindy's mind reeled. She was devastated. She had loaned Ann her car. Had the car's brakes failed? How was that possible? The car, a Honda Civic, was a year old and had just had a tune up the month before. It didn't make any sense.

The nurse looked over at her, troubled.

"Do you have someone else who can come in and keep you company? A husband, or boyfriend or something?"

The truth hit Cindy at that moment.

"No," she said quietly, "I have no one."

The nurse shook her head, "I'm sorry."

Then she pulled the curtains and walked out of the cubicle.

Ann looked peaceful resting there, and Cindy didn't want to make her talk. She was breathing on her own, that was good. There was a brace around her neck. Probably the usual precaution after a car accident.

"Stay awake, Ann," Cindy said, gently nudging her. Ann's eyes fluttered opened.

Cindy held her sister's hand and tried to settle down . Was it possible, she wondered, that Ann would die? It was much more than she could bear. She held onto Ann's hand for dear life. "You're gonna make it," Cindy whispered to her, over and over. "Just keep breathing, Ann. Help is here. You're not alone." She felt Ann's pulse calm down as she spoke to her, as if her very cells heard what Cindy said.

Then the curtains were pulled open again and the nurse returned to tell her that the police wanted to talk to her.

Reluctantly, Cindy got up and left her bedside.

Outside, in the waiting room, a rugged-looking officer in his late forties was standing, waiting for her.

"Cindy Blaine?" he asked, looking down at a notepad.

Cindy followed him to some benches in the hallway, where they both sat down. The hospital was crowded with patients and families, walking back and forth, along with doctors, nurses, technicians wheeling trays.

Cindy looked over at him and was surprised to see his hazel eyes looking at her searchingly.

"What happened to my sister?" she asked.

"The car veered off the road and hit a tree. She banged her head against the windshield. It didn't break. Could have been much worse. There was no sign of alcohol. Does your sister take drugs?"

"Not at all."

"Not to your knowledge?"

"Not at all."

"Not even for medical purposes?"

"No, she doesn't. "

"The rain was strong and the roads were slippery," he said. "The car is relatively new. It's registered to you?"

"Yes. She told me the brakes gave out. Is that true?"

The officer looked at her.

"Could be. We'll have to do a run up on it. Did you ever have any trouble with it?"

"No."

"Your sister lives with you?"

"No. She lives in Wisconsin with her husband. She's been here for a visit."

"For how long?"

Cindy thought that was an odd question. What did it matter? "She's been here for a while," Cindy said.

"Trouble at home?" he asked.

"No," Cindy replied. "She came to help me. My husband died recently."

He stopped writing, and seemed really taken aback . "I'm really sorry."

"An accident on our honeymoon," Cindy continued. Suddenly she had an intense desire to tell him everything. She so badly wanted someone to talk to. To tell him her suspicions about Clint's accident. About her in-laws. The suspicious photo. Could there be a connection with all this and the car accident? Her in-laws had access to her garage. Had someone tampered with the brakes? They would have thought it was Cindy driving. Was this accident meant for her?

Who wanted her dead? And why? And what did it have to do with Clint?

"Is it possible that my car was tampered with?" she asked, tentatively.

He looked her over.

"Why do you ask that?"

"I…" she began. But she didn't know what to say. It was all too overwhelming.

"My husband's death…I don't think it was an accident."

He stared at her.

"How did he die?"

"In the ocean. Surfing. In Barbados."

Tears filled Cindy's eyes.

"He wasn't meant to die," she simply said, and despite herself, started to cry.

"And my car was in perfect shape. It had to be someone close by who messed with the brakes, someone with access to my garage."

She felt his hand on her shoulder.

"Lady," he said, "you've been through a lot. I think you should go home and rest. We'll do a full diagnostic on your car. Don't worry. If anything's out of place, you'll be the first to know. OK?"

But as she watched him leave, as she stood there alone in the waiting room, she suddenly knew - without a doubt. Clint's death and the car incident were related. That accident was meant for her. She was more convinced than ever that whoever wanted Clint dead, wanted her dead, too.

And that they'd stop at nothing until that happened.

Chapter 9

Ann was diagnosed with a concussion, whiplash and a broken collarbone. They monitored her closely. This should have been me, Cindy kept thinking. I'm not supposed to be alive. For some odd reason, it didn't surprise her, just woke her up and raised the ante. If she wanted to keep on living, she'd *have* to find out what was going on.

Cindy stayed at her sister's bedside, holding her hand as they moved her to her own room . Above all, she was determined for Ann to get well. "You're going to be fine," she kept murmuring, as though it were a mantra.

Once Ann arrived in her room, Cindy had to sit on a chair in the corner as the nurses took over, moved Ann to a hospital bed, took her vital signs, set up her medication. As she sat there watching, Cindy turned the events over in her head.

No question about it, what happened in Barbados was far from over. Everything that happened since then was linked by a silver thread. Cindy had to trace that thread, pull on it a little, and everything would open up. The hostility with Clint's family hadn't ended, only grown worse. They were the only ones she knew that had access to her garage. They had to think it would be her driving. And who else would have that photo?

As Cindy traced the silver thread it kept pointing to the family again and again. And what about Clint? They were furious that he disregarded their advice about the marriage. Had one of them arranged for him to be kidnapped and killed when he went down to the beach? Was his body dumped on shore so it could be found and the case closed? Who had to gain most by that?

Cindy thought about Marge's husband Ralph - how silent and sullen he usually was. Was he afraid that Clint's marriage to Cindy would affect his position in the family or his inheritance? He'd come from a poor family, was obsessed with financial security. She wouldn't put it past him. And Marge and Clint were never close .

Is that why Clint would never talk about the family? Could he have realized there was danger and not let it on? Had he kept all kinds of secrets from her? The idea of it horrified her, but she had to face the possibility, whether she liked it or not. The photo told her that something shady was lurking in his past. Was it possible that someone had a vendetta against him?

Cindy felt her world start to shake, as though there was no longer solid ground to stand on. She could not rest until she found out what really happened. Nothing else mattered anymore.

The door to the hospital room opened, and in walked Ann's husband, Frank.

He had just flow in from Wisconsin, and he looked exhausted and frightened.

He and Cindy had never gotten on well. She'd always been an annoyance to him, seemed to take up too much of Ann's time.

From his expression, it looked like he held Cindy responsible for Ann's injuries .

Frank was a tall, heavy set man, who was street smart, did well in business, and cared deeply about his wife. He ran into the room the minute he got there to see Ann, barely saying hello to Cindy.

Cindy got up and went into the hall, to give them time alone together.

Standing in the hall, she thought how she never understood how Ann could have chosen Frank, or why the two of them were so close, but she was happy for her.

Cindy's heart contracted as she felt how much she missed Clint . If he had been here, Ann would never have gotten hurt. Clint would have picked up Frank at the airport and by now, the four of them would be going out for Chinese food. Clint had always liked Frank. The emptiness Cindy felt gripped her deeply. How would she ever get over this? She wouldn't.

She suddenly realized that it didn't matter. Maybe it wasn't about ever getting over it. It was about finding the truth, getting justice for Clint, stopping worse things from happening. There was no time for self-pity. She had a big job ahead.

When Frank finally came out into the hall, his face looked ashen. He actually looked older than Cindy had remembered.

"I'm so sorry about this, Frank," Cindy said to him.

He just grunted.

"Ann will be fine."

"Of course she'll be fine," he said briskly. "She has to stay in the hospital a while though. Then there will be rehab. This is a nightmare."

"I don't know how it happened," Cindy murmured.

"What do you mean you don't know? Your brakes failed. Didn't you have your car checked?"

"It's almost new. And I did."

"Hell," Frank couldn't stand talking to her, "there's always something happening around you, isn't there?"

Cindy resented his comment. "Are you blaming me for the accident?"

"I'm not blaming anyone. I just said, there's always something. It gets exhausting."

"I'm sorry, Frank."

"Sorry isn't enough. I don't see why you don't just come back to Wisconsin when your sister's better and give her some peace of mind?"

"I can't. Not until I find out who killed Clint."

Frank stopped cold in his tracks then. "You got to be kidding?"

"He didn't die surfing."

"What in hell are you talking about now? Did the police tell you something?"

"No. They don't have to. I just know."

"Know what?" Frank's eyes were spinning. He was beginning to look ill.

"You know how the family couldn't bear anyone of Clint's girlfriends," said Cindy.

"And?" Frank looked terrified.

"How do you think they felt about me taking him away from them for good? Just think about it for a minute."

"Oh Jesus," Frank called out. "You're going nuts."

"Whoever killed him, wants me dead, too. If I go back to Wisconsin, they'll hunt me down there, too."

"You're completely crazy - paranoid!" he said.

"Just the opposite. I'm on the trail of something big. But I'm not safe anywhere until I find them. And, if I came to Wisconsin, you and Ann won't be safe either."

"You're worse than I thought," Frank finally uttered.

Then he suddenly made a beeline for the bathroom down the hall.

Cindy watched him run down the hall as the nurse came out of Ann's room and tapped her on the shoulder.

"Come back in, this minute" she said, "your sister's breathing is labored. She needs you there."

*

Cindy sat at Ann's side while she struggled for air. The sound of Ann's breathing reminded Cindy of the strange birds she'd heard on Barbados, cawing through the trees in the dark of night. For a few moments, she wondered if complications were arising that could not be handled. Would Ann die?

Frank was nowhere to be found. After throwing up, he needed a break, and went downstairs to pace back and forth on the city streets. By the time he returned, things quieted down, and Cindy could leave the hospital. It was the middle of the night.

As Cindy walked through the deserted hospital parking lot, on her way to Clint's small car, she suddenly heard footsteps.

She turned and searched the dimly lit lot, and felt a rush of fear race through her. Were they following her?

The footsteps grew louder, and Cindy hid behind a cement column. She watched and waited.

Finally, he came into a view. It was just a doctor, heading to his car.

Cindy breathed a huge sigh of relief. She chastised herself. Was she really losing it?

When Cindy got home, she could not get to sleep.

She rolled over in bed and took the Bible Tom Mallord had given her. She opened it randomly and began to read:

For whatever is hidden is meant to be disclosed, and what is concealed is meant to be brought out into the open.

Cindy sat up straight. That was beautiful. It was a sign. It was encouraging her to go forward, telling her the truth would be revealed .

If anyone has ears to hear, let him hear.

Cindy shivered. She had ears to hear. Her ears, her mind, her heart had all been ripped open. She was listening with every pore of her body. Waiting to hear the next steps to take.

Chapter 10

Cindy couldn't go to Philadelphia and speak to Heather directly until she knew Ann was stable. And it was going to be a long haul. Complications were setting in, Ann was having congestion in her lungs and being closely monitored. Frank was at her side constantly, but Cindy was afraid to leave town, even for a few hours.

"Go do what you have to," Frank told her. "You're not helping your sister by staying here looking like death warmed over. Do what you have to feel better. I've got things under control."

Cindy knew he felt better without her there, but there was truth in what he said as well. What good was it to Ann or anyone, if more trouble was about to happen and there was no one trying to stop it?

Before she started the day, Cindy decided it was time to take a good, long run to clear her head . She'd been cooped up inside for far too long. She dressed quickly in shorts and a T shirt and decided to take Clint's small car and drive down to Arbor Lane to jog.

It was the first time Cindy was out of the house in three weeks. As she drove through town to Arbor Lane, she looked at the winding, cobblestone, tree lined streets. Cove Bay was a quaint suburb. Both the town and people in it were well-groomed, charming and reassuring. There was a large clock in the center of town and benches under it . Small, charming, upscale shops and outdoor cafes lined the streets . People were walking up and down, doing errands, talking, as if everything were normal, as if another murder had not almost been committed, right in their midst.

Cindy drove past a Ben and Jerry's and a large music store. At the far corner of the next block was a sports store and art supply shop. Clint had had every advantage growing up here, safe and secure. He'd loved Cove Bay and had been determined to settle here and raise a family. Initially Cindy had suggested that they move a little further away from the family, to the next town over. But he was adamant on this point. He would never leave Cove Bay.

It felt strange to be driving through his town now without him, almost as if she were a ghost passing through his world.

She turned in another direction and drove down the back streets to Arbor Road.

Arbor Road was a beautiful, deserted, tree lined road that led down to the bay. Very few even knew about the road or came down to the bay. Clint had taken her there to run many times. It was perfect for jogging and clearing her head. And it was great to sit on one of the large rocks on the jetties when she got there. She could sit and listen to the sound of water splashing and decide what move to make next.

She parked under a tree and got out. The horror of having Ann in the hospital came over her in waves . She kept seeing Ann laying there helpless, reaching out for her hand.

The sweet smell of Wisterias filled the air, along with the salty smell of the water. Cindy took a few delicious breaths. It wouldn't do Ann any good for Cindy to become immobilized. The best thing she could do for Ann now was to stay healthy and vigilant.

Cindy began to jog down towards the end of the road . It felt amazing to be moving again. The air caressed her face as she jogged by, reassuring her that there was beauty in life, that she could go on.

The trees on both sides made an arbor for her, supporting her along her way. It was easy to lose herself jogging, and forget everything. For a moment, she wanted to forget, too. Co-workers from her office kept calling. They missed her. Even though she had all the time she needed, they hoped she could come back for even a day or two.

Part of Cindy wanted to go back to work, pretend the world was safe and normal, resume life as usual, become one of the people doing errands in town.

Jogging now along the road, Cindy had a flash of desire not to stir up anymore mess. She wanted to believe Clint's death was really an accident. Then she could spend time with Ann in the hospital until she was better, go to work at the paper, lunch with friends, take in a movie at night. She could get a lawyer to deal with Clint's family and start her life all over again.

She jogged a little faster then, excited and scared at the thought. Ann was right in a funny way. Time would pass and heal her wounds. But what about Clint? Would his wounds ever heal? How could his life count for nothing? He deserved better. He deserved justice, and she deserved to know the truth.

And, besides, what made her think the killing was over? Right this very minute, she felt it was likely that someone wanted her dead. She'd been too close to Clint. It had to be messy having her still around.

No, there was no turning back. Her work was cut out for her, whether she liked it or not.

It was about nine o'clock when she got to the bay, and the morning sun was coming up. She stopped and stretched under a tree, and found a big, slippery rock to rest on. Just as she climbed up on it, she saw a figure walking towards her on the sand. He wore running shorts, with a towel around his neck and looked familiar and friendly. As he got closer, she was surprised to see Al, Clint's best man.

"My God, is that you, Cindy?" he said, coming closer, breathing hard.

Cindy couldn't have been more surprised. He stopped there on the sand, in front of the rock, looking up at her. "What in the world are you doing here?" he said.

"I went for a jog. Clint and I always jogged here."

"Good for you," he said. "Good. It's amazing you can get back to jogging." Then he looked across the sand and down at the water. "I want to tell you again," he said, "how sorry I am, how awful. Everyone's still talking about it."

"Thanks," Cindy said, covering her eyes from the glare of the sun.

"I mean Clint was the most extraordinary guy."

"I know," Cindy said.

"Boy am I glad I got to spend that day with Clint at the end of March. I keep thinking about it. We had a wonderful time."

Cindy's mind raced. "The end of March?" She didn't remember Clint mentioning anything about spending a day with Al in March. She reviewed Clint's schedule in her mind again.

He'd gone to a conference in Washington, D.C. during a week-end in March. Other than that, he'd been with her. She'd had no idea that Al had been at the conference as well.

"Oh yes," she said, "I remember, the conference in Washington, D.C."

"In Boston," Al repeated, "the end of March. We didn't go to a conference, just had a great time."

Cindy was silent. Al looked at her strangely. "You've got a lot on your mind," he said. "It's easy to forget stuff like that."

"Very easy," she replied. She had no intention of letting him know that she knew nothing about it. Or that all kinds of lies were piling up fast.

"We went to the Grande Hotel. He must have told you."

"Of course," Cindy said. "There are just so many details to think of now."

"Sure," Al said. "Really, I'm sorry."

Clint never told her he was going to the Grande Hotel with anyone in March. Despite the warm sun overhead, a long chill went through her spine.

Al knew Clint since they were kids. Cindy suddenly wanted to ask him about Heather Krane, but thought better of it. If she told him about the photo, it would spread all over town. That was the last thing Cindy wanted.

"I knew Clint for such a long time," Al said then.

"I'd love to learn more," Cindy said. "It's natural to want to know about Clint's life when he was young and growing up."

"Of course it is," Al said, "It makes you feel closer to him now."

"Right," Cindy said. "I only knew him a year before we married—"

"We all know that," he interrupted. "No one could get over it. That family of his, they're an interesting bunch. And Clint was their golden boy. They didn't take too well to his girlfriends. Not a one of them. The guys always joked about it. We couldn't believe they actually let him get married. We heard that you and Marge got along great."

Al put his towel down and started stretching.

Clint had probably told him that. It was Clint's favorite fantasy. She'd tried to tell Clint how hard his family was on her, but he couldn't hear it, always thought they were getting along great. Cindy had thought it wouldn't matter so much, once she and Clint were married. She couldn't believe how wrong she'd been.

She was relieved when Al left and she could sit alone and figure out what had just happened. He and Clint had been in Boston for a day in March? What in the world was he was talking about? She ruffled through the few past months in her mind again. There was no question, Clint had only been out of town once, at the end of March to a conference on offshore drilling in Washington, D. C. He'd written a paper to present at it .

Something was terribly off. She got up from the rock, brushed herself off, and started back, eager to check Clint's records and calendar. There had to be receipts from the trip, notes, memorandums. It was part of Clint's job.

*

The minute she got home she went right into his office.

It was amazing to see how much stuff was packed into Clint's drawers. There were also plenty of files in the unopened boxes in the back of the room that hadn't been sorted out yet .

As Cindy ruffled through Clint's papers she found different calendars from years gone by, all crumpled together. She put them in another pile, shocked at how messy everything was. She kept her records clearly and simply. When something was over, she threw it away. Her calendar was for this year only.

She waded through one calendar of his after another and finally, dug out the one for this past March. The conference in Washington, D.C. was written on it. Cindy sighed a sigh of relief. But then her eyes were drawn to the bottom of the page. There was a note in red ink that said his presentation had been cancelled. Cindy gasped. He'd never told her that. She scoured through this page and others to see any mention of Boston, or the Hotel Grande. Not a word. She was sure that Clint was gone that week-end, though, and that he told her he was going to the conference in Washington, D.C.

Cindy sat back in the wooden chair and put her head in her hands. A sharp pain ran through her right temple. There was no doubt about it, Clint had lied, perhaps again and again. She was suddenly frightened to go further. What else she would find? More than anything in the world, she had trusted Clint completely, and told him so many times. He'd smiled when she said that.

"You can trust me with everything," he'd said. "I'll always be here for you."

Was she an idiot? She felt as though she hadn't really known the man she married. Had he been living his life on a slippery slope?

She got up for a moment, went to the bathroom and splashed cold water on her face. It was easy to doubt everything now, to be afraid to trust her judgment ever again. But Cindy refused to. There was definitely a part of his world he was hiding, but she didn't know why. Maybe he needed some time away with his friends and didn't know how to ask for it? She had to be careful before thinking the worst. She had to be tough with herself now. It was time to gather facts. She had to see where the silver thread really lead her. This was no time for playing head games.

Cindy would have to go over every paper of his, see how he lived, what he was up to, what he had to hide. And who would have wanted him dead . She couldn't wait until Ann got out of the hospital. Too much was happening too fast. But first, she had to see Heather in person. And she had to do it today.

Chapter 11

Cindy, in Clint's small car, headed to Philadelphia. She was determined to meet Heather face to face. She needed to know whatever Heather could tell her.

Before she left, Cindy had dialed Heather's number, just to see if she was there. A light voice had answered.

"Hi, who's there?"

Cindy had hung up. She was there, she was home. That was all Cindy needed to know.

The drive was quick and easy. The car almost flew on its own. When she got down to Philadelphia, she checked the map and followed the streets that curved around until she found Heather's block .

Heather lived in a three story brownstone on a residential, tree lined street. Cindy pulled up and parked right across from her house. She'd planned to get out of the car as soon as she got there, go to the door, ring the bell and introduce herself . But suddenly she thought better of it. Cindy had no idea how Heather would react. She could close the door in Cindy's face. If

Cindy refused to leave, she could call the police. Cindy couldn't risk that. She *had to* confront Heather in person, show her the photo, ask her about it directly.

It was just about lunch time. Cindy decided to wait in the car, across the street, and keep her eye on the brownstone until Heather came out. Cindy was prepared to sit there and wait all day, or even all night long if need be. When Heather came out, Cindy would follow her in the car, see where she went. At the perfect moment, when Heather was alone, Cindy would get out, go over to her, and show her the photo.

After about half an hour of watching the house, Cindy began to wonder what would happen if Heather came out surrounded by friends? They might all be going to lunch. And, when Cindy did confront Heather, what if she couldn't get her to talk? It was also possible that she would lie. Cindy was convinced she was sharp enough, though, to pick up on that.

Cindy turned on the radio. The station was playing oldies. She flipped to another station, news. Restless, Cindy turned it off . Just at that moment, the door to Heather's brownstone opened and out she came, with a little boy in a stroller. She carefully pushed the stroller down the front stairs, one step at a time. It was shocking to see her in person, like this. Just as in the photo, she was tall and beautiful. Dressed in jeans and a polo shirt, she seemed happy and carefree, going about her normal day.

Cindy wanted to jump out of the car and race up to her, but she knew she couldn't yet. Instead, she followed her in the car, slowly down the block, watching her every move. Heather went to the corner, crossed and then walked another few blocks. Cindy trailed along. Oblivious to the fact that a car was following her, Heather chatted lightly with her son.

When she got to the third corner, Heather turned to the right and headed for a children's playground. Except for a few mothers and children, scattered here and there, the place was mostly empty.

Cindy parked across from the playground and watched.

Heather went in through the open gates, unstrapped her son from the stroller. He squirmed out right away, and ran to the swings. She went running after him, laughing and then picking him up to put him in a swing.

Cindy felt a mixture of sorrow and pain. This was the life she should have been living.

She got out of the car slowly and walked into the playground. Then she sat down on the bench opposite the swings and watched Heather swing her son.

Even though it was late Spring, a cool breeze blew up. Heather was beautiful and playful. Cindy's heart clenched into a knot. Had Clint loved her? Were they still seeing each other when he died? Were they emailing? Had he ever gotten over her?

Cindy got up then, went over to the swings and stood next to Heather and her son.

"Hi," Cindy said lightly.

Heather looked right at her. "Hi," she smiled, "Do I know you?"

Cindy couldn't find the words to answer. She decided to go straight to the point, reached into her pocket and pulled the photo out.

"Someone sent this to me in the mail," Cindy said, showing her the photo.

"Oh my God," Heather said, staring at it. "A picture of me?"

"And your son."

"I never saw this photo," she looked at it more closely, puzzled. "I didn't even know it was taken. Who sent it to you? Who are you?"

"To be more exact, they sent it to my husband," said Cindy.

Heather became ill at ease. "What has this got to do with me?" she said.

Cindy felt badly. She liked her, and was sorry to have to put her through this.

"Someone killed my husband," Cindy said bluntly.

Heather gasped. "That's horrible."

The little child in the swing began calling out for more. Heather had stopped swinging him. She was standing there, transfixed.

"Clint Blaine was my husband," said Cindy.

"Clint Blaine's dead?" Heather breathed. For a moment it looked as if she would buckle. It was hard for her to stand up . "Oh my God. I hadn't heard."

Cindy believed her. "Let's go sit on the bench and talk."

"Swing me higher, swing me higher," the little boy kept calling.

Heather ignored him.

"Someone send Clint this picture a week before our wedding" Cindy said.

"Can you tell me why?"

"I have no idea," said Heather, "I don't know who even took it. I haven't seen Clint for at least three years."

"You're friends on Facebook," Cindy said.

"I have eleven hundred friends," Heather was talking fast. "I friended him a long time ago, just for the heck of it. I haven't kept up with his life. When did the two of you get married?"

"A little over a month ago," said Cindy.

"I never heard anything so awful," she said.

Her boy called out again: "Mommy! Mommy!"

"He's a beautiful child," Cindy said. She looked at him closely now, for the first time. He had huge blue eyes, just like Clint, and a mischievous smile.

"There's something you're not telling me," Cindy said slowly. "And it's the reason I have this photo."

Heather began trembling, as if a cold frost had blown in.

"I don't even know you," she said in a thin voice.

"You can check me out on Facebook," said Cindy. "You'll see I was Clint's wife. What reason would I have to lie? Was something going on between the two of you?"

"It was no big deal. It was over three years ago," Heather said. "We dated a little and that was about it. It didn't mean that much to me, or him either. Right when I was dating him, I met someone else and really fell in love. It was the man I married. Clint and I broke up shortly after . We were casual friends afterwards for a couple of months, and that was it."

The two women stared at each other. "I swear it," said Heather.

Cindy knew in her gut that wasn't the whole story.

"You have to tell me everything," Cindy said, "because now I'm in danger, and so is my family."

Heather could barely speak. "It's awful, really awful," she finally uttered, taking it in.

"You have to tell me the truth. Did you see Clint this past year?" Cindy steeled herself for anything.

"Not at all," Heather gasped . "I swear to you, I'm happily married."

"Did he contact you?" said Cindy.

"Not once. There was no reason."

"Swing more mamma!" the child called out.

"Heather, listen, there's a reason someone sent Clint your photo a few weeks before he was killed."

Heather blanched.

"The killing's not all over, either," Cindy went on. "Not by a long shot. We all could be in danger."

Heather looked terrified. "What do you mean, *we*?"

"Whoever killed Clint took this photo of you and your son."

"My son could be in danger?" She started trembling.

"Anything's possible," Cindy said.

Heather's eyes filled with tears. "You have to swear you won't tell anybody," the words poured out of her. "Swear." She was trembling.

"I don't know if I can swear," said Cindy. "I may have to tell someone if you and your son need protection."

"I have no idea who took the picture, but this is Clint's child," Heather burst out. "Nobody knows it. Not even Clint. I never told him. I never told my husband either. He thinks the child is his. We were so happy together, we were getting married, it would have ruined everything. I didn't know myself who the father was, at first. The timing of everything overlapped. It was crazy."

"How did you find out it was Clint's child?"

"He looks so much like him," Heather's voice was shaky. "I look at him and see Clint. I couldn't stand it, so I finally had him tested. Just to be sure."

Cindy's feelings were all over the place. She and Clint had often spoken about the family they wanted to have together. Now Clint had a child that he never knew, with someone else. That was awful. On the other hand, there was a part of Clint still alive. That was wonderful.

"I've got to keep my son safe, and also my marriage." Heather couldn't catch her breath. Then she started sobbing.

Cindy wanted to calm Heather down. "It must be so painful for you to keep all this hidden," she said .

"No, it isn't," Heather said. "I love my son. I love my husband. My husband loves the child as his own. I'll have more children later on. Who's hurt by this? Nobody."

"But somebody knows," Cindy said.

Heather's eyes opened wide. "Who?"

"The person who took the photo."

"They want to ruin my life?" said Heather, "Why?"

The two women stood beside one another, sudden compatriots, facing an unknown enemy.

"They wanted to ruin Clint's life," Cindy answered.

"But why?"

"That's what I'm trying to figure out," said Cindy. "But I believe that whoever took the photo, killed Clint as well."

It was too much for Heather. She put her hands over her face.

"I'm terrified," she murmured.

Cindy wanted to soothe her but didn't know how.

"Swing me more mamma, swing me more!" the little boy cried out, lifting his arms up to the sky.

*

Driving back to New York, Cindy's mind was spinning. It had stunned her to find out about Clint's son. If Heather was just a casual girlfriend, and if he had no idea about the child, there was no reason why Clint should have mentioned her. She had no choice but to believe Heather.

But who could know about the child? Who wanted Clint alerted? His family knew about all his girlfriends. Had someone in the family managed to track all this down? Take the photo? Who else would even care? For a crazy moment, Cindy wondered if her marriage to Clint could have ever worked? Suddenly, she wasn't sure. There were so many unknown clouds floating around him, so many dark corners in his life.

She didn't know if she could bear finding another one, could bear losing the memory of the man she'd so deeply loved.

Chapter 12

When Cindy got home, she was exhausted. She made herself a cup of tea and collapsed on the sofa, drinking it slowly, thinking about Clint's son. Clint would have been a wonderful father. Cindy felt awful that Clint would never see him, never even know that a woman he barely knew was the mother of his child.

Then out of nowhere, the doorbell rang. *It must be another package*, Cindy thought. Wedding gifts were still arriving daily from people who hadn't heard what happened yet.

Cindy got up and went to the door.

It was Clint's mother.

It was extremely unusual for Clint's family to just drop by. And his mother couldn't have picked a worse time. Cindy was not in the mood to see her.

And beside her stood Marge, looking distraught.

"We need to talk to you."

They marched into the living room without asking and scanned the place, up and down. Cindy wondered what they were looking for.

"I never knew why Clint chose this house," his mother said bitterly. It was an old story, Cindy'd heard it many times.

"Because he loved this house," Cindy said briskly. "And so did I."

"Clint loved all kinds of odd things," Clint's mother looked at Cindy through half closed eyes. "He didn't always have the best taste."

Cindy didn't really have energy for this.

"There was a lot in Clint's life that we didn't understand," said Marge.

"Sit," Cindy said perfunctorily. "It's been a busy day."

"Really?" said Marge. "What did you do?"

Cindy resented any question at all from them about her personal life. She decided to push the envelope now, as she was sick of pretending all was normal.

"I've been checking on some leads I have," Cindy said, matter of factly.

"What kind of leads?" his mother perked up.

"Leads about who might have had Clint killed."

Both Marge and his mother shuddered. Cindy knew it was harsh, but she was tired of games.

"I'm delving more and more into Clint's life," Cindy continued, and looked at both of them closely. "There's a lot that doesn't add up."

His mother peered back. "Whatever Clint did or didn't have in his life, he didn't deserve to die."

Cindy met her head on. "No one deserves to die. And no one deserves to be a young widow either."

"You're hardly a widow," Clint's mother snapped. "You two weren't even married a week. More like a girlfriend."

Cindy felt punched in the heart. She couldn't let this go on.

"I am Clint's wife," she retorted, "We were married on May 18th, in full view of friends and family. Even if you didn't like it. And I have the papers to prove it."

"What is and isn't legal is a big question regarding marriage these days," Marge replied.

Cindy began to feel nauseous. "You're bigger than the law?" Cindy said, "think you can do whatever you like?"

"What do you mean by that?" said his mother.

"Richard knows all about these matters," Marge continued. "He's a wonderful husband and wonderful lawyer . We've been talking it all over."

Clint's mother nodded avidly. She suddenly looked frail and pathetic, clutching a huge, patent leather bag. In that moment, Cindy felt sorry for her. She wanted to bring her tea. After all, she had lost her son.

But his mother continued, on the attack. "I want you to tell me why there wasn't anyone there to rescue my son? It doesn't make sense. The time of death listed on the Coroner's report was just a few minutes before you got down to the beach."

That odd fact gripped Cindy again. She didn't know what to make of it, or how the time had been determined. It left her weak in the knees, imagining Clint dying and then her arriving a few moments later.

"You took our son away from the family, and now he's never coming back."

Cindy felt the blood drain from her face. "It's convenient, isn't it, blaming me?"

"I have no idea what you're talking about," said Marge. "And neither does anyone in the family. We don't understand you. Never have. Never will."

Cindy would never think of these people as her family. She had no idea how Clint could have died and left her here with them.

"Where were you this afternoon?" Clint's mother asked her. "We were calling and calling."

"What difference does it make?" said Cindy.

"The insurance company has contacted us and the Will has to be probated."

Why would the insurance company contact them, Cindy wondered?

"My father is very ill," Marge added. "Big decisions need to be made."

They're here because they're worried about money, Cindy realized. *They haven't once asked me how I'm feeling.*

Clint's mother spoke up tensely, "Everyone knows that Clint was headstrong and foolish at times in the past. He'd made some poor choices. Now we have to sort those choices out."

"I always knew Clint to be completely upright in every way," Cindy said. "Was I wrong? Are there things no one is telling me?"

"That's the whole point of it, isn't it?" His mother's face grew tighter. "You only knew him for a short while. We knew him his entire life long. We knew every little thing about him, his friends, his lovers, his mistakes. What did you really know? Very little."

They were trying to shake her total confidence - that was their tactic . She wouldn't allow it.

"We need to discuss what happens with the insurance and the house," Marge shot in .

Now that Clint was gone, Marge probably wanted to get her fair share.

"What's to discuss? Cindy said. "The house belongs to me."

"The house is in my son's name alone," Clint's mother corrected her.

Cindy was shocked. She hadn't realized that. She thought Clint had put it in both their names.

"We gave him money for the down payment with the agreement that he would put it exclusively in his name."

Cindy didn't know that they gave him the down payment. He'd led her to believe that he had plenty of funds on his own.

"Well, I am his wife," Cindy said, "so the house automatically goes to me."

"Nothing is automatic," Marge replied. "It depends on the Will."

"You want to take the house away from me?" Cindy was shocked.

"It doesn't rightfully belong to you," said Marge. "The house belonged to Clint. And he belonged to us."

Cindy's faced flushed .

"Clint didn't rightfully belong to you either," Clint's mother spat out. "Who knows how you wrapped him around your little finger? You met and were married in less than a year. That wasn't like Clint."

Clearly, the family was building a case.

"It seems as if I need a lawyer," Cindy said .

"You need more than a lawyer," Marge continued. "You need to get out of here. Go home. Clear out. This is too painful to all of us, having you so close by. Then we'll let lawyers decide about who gets the house and how the insurance settlement will be divided up."

Cindy couldn't leave the house, even if she wanted to. Clint was there. He belonged to her .

"I suppose you're claiming that you gave Clint money for the insurance policy as well?" she said.

"Not claiming. We have evidence of it. Signed checks and receipts. Compensation is due us. Fair is fair."

Cindy couldn't take another second of this. "I'll tell you what's fair," she finally burst out, livid. "It's fair for me to have in-laws who care about me! It's fair for you to realize that your precious son got married and didn't belong to you! Who knows how he really died? Did it enrage you so much to actually lose him, that you arranged it yourself?"

Marge gasped. "You're evil and insane."

Cindy went on, only half in control. "I'm checking it all out. Including you!"

"Why would we kill our own child?" Clint's mother began to heave. "We came to make you an offer. The law is completely on our side. Instead of leaving you with nothing, we're offering you money if you just get out of town. It's too painful for us to see you here. It keeps reminding us of what happened to him."

Cindy fell back, silent on the couch. "You want to pay me to leave?"

"Please," his mother said. "We'll make it worth your while."

"Aren't there easier ways to get rid of me?" Cindy looked right at her.

She seemed confused. "I don't know what you're talking about."

Cindy realized that she didn't. When she looked over at Marge, she saw her gnawing on her lower lip.

At that moment, seeing how pathetic and helpless they were, she suddenly realized. She realized, without a doubt, that, however sick these people were, they were ultimately powerless, incapable of having Clint killed.

The realization struck Cindy hard. She had been barking up the wrong tree all this time. His family had nothing to do with it after all. Which meant that whoever had done it was still out there, still after her. And whoever that was, she'd better figure it out quick.

Chapter 13

When Clint's family left, Cindy stood staring out of the window, wishing she could speak to Clint. He'd always shown her the bigger picture, helped her know what to do. If something had bothered her, he'd just put his arms around her and they'd thrash it out. After that, they'd spent the rest of the time in each other's arms. It had made the whole world right.

Now, she was alone with everything. There were important decisions to be made. Leaving was out of the question. It wasn't the house itself she was attached to—it was the feeling of Clint in it, everywhere. Where else could she go to be close to him now?

The visit with his family this afternoon had turned things around, though. Cindy knew Clint's family was wealthy, but up to now, she didn't know Clint took anything from them. He told her he'd paid for the wedding and the down payment on the house . She'd believed it, believed everything he'd said. She'd felt she'd found a soul mate, after years of rough times with guys.

She needed answers. Even though she was exhausted, Cindy went back into Clint's study. She turned on a light and looked at the huge mess of papers. It would be a long night.

She pulled papers out of Clint's desk and sorted them; there were old bills, faxes from work, receipts from restaurants. There was a receipt for the deposit he'd sent to the hotel they'd stayed at for the honeymoon. She picked it up and held it to her face to see if she could still smell the salty air. She couldn't. She put it down and kept taking other papers out of the drawers and arranging them in piles.

Most of the bills and receipts were easy to recognize. Some were for business. Cindy put those in a pile. Then she found a receipt from the Grande Hotel in Boston, for the week-end Clint was supposed to be in D.C . She put that receipt on her lap. It confirmed what Al told her. She didn't like it, but it wasn't a shock .

The next receipt she found, though, stopped her completely. It was from a hotel in Manhattan, Century Plaza, dated three weeks before the wedding. Cindy's heart started pounding. There had to be an explanation, though she didn't know what.

She'd contact Clint's old assistant, Bara, who had his full schedule at work .

She put that receipt in a separate place and continued. She wasn't sure exactly what she was looking for either, but knew she'd recognize it when it came around. It was the tapestry of a life she was touching, of days, hours, money spent, calls received and answered.

When all the drawers of the desk were cleared, she went to Clint's computer to check through his personal emails and files. It was strange typing his password and logging in. Even though she knew she had to do it, Cindy felt as though she were invading his private life. It made her think of her own emails. She knew there were probably dozens of them piling up. But she just hadn't been able to deal with them.

There were 180 emails waiting for Clint. It was going to be a long night. Cindy began opening them, one at a time. There were emails about meetings scheduled, and attended. She read follow up comments from Clint and thank you notes from others to him for his terrific contribution. There were invitations for lunch, dinner . There were even a few emails from a lobbyist. Clint had had a busy life.

Cindy knew he went to Washington regularly and attended conferences, but didn't realize that he'd also met with lobbyists. She hadn't known the full extent of his research, or that it impacted on bills passed in Congress. Clint had only mentioned it once or twice in passing.

There were a bunch of emails from a guy named Greg Hamden, a close co-worker of Clint's. Cindy remembered him mentioning

Greg. He and Clint had been working on the Tearwall Project together for a while.

The emails from Greg were right to the point.

Got the info, Clint. Thanks. Talk later.

Cindy kept scrolling through the emails to see if she could find more.

Another one gave her pause for a moment -

Can't believe you're finally getting married. She better be worthy of you. And, she better know what she's getting into. Signed A.V.

Clint hadn't responded to that one. What was it Cindy didn't know that she was getting into, that A.V. knew?

Cindy kept scrolling. There were a cluster of emails talking about the Washington Conference. Clint had been excited to go. He was presenting a paper on the Tearwall Project . He'd written a bunch of emails telling people the time and place of his presentation, that he was looking forward to seeing them there.

Then something had happened. There were a flurry of emails from people at his company asking Clint to come to meetings. He and Greg had met for separate lunches. Clint's presentation had suddenly been cancelled. Cindy couldn't tear herself away. Clint had told her he'd gone to the conference and presented his paper there.

The emails told a different story .

When the presentation was cancelled, Clint, very upset, emailed Greg to let him know.

Jesus Christ was all Greg answered .

Unbelievable, Clint wrote back.

Be smart, Greg replied.

Cindy didn't know what to make of all this. She needed more information about the Tearwall Project and why Clint's presentation had been tossed aside. She also realized she needed more information about his company and what exactly it was involved in.

Cindy went to the company's public website . She clicked on the company history and its employees and a whole page devoted to Clint came up.

Clint's function in the company was to investigate the environmental and ecological effects of a drill at a particular location. To advise the company of the safety parameters involved. He was also a prominent part of the public relations effort of the firm. It felt good reading about him, seeing how important he was to them.

There were several pieces about him posted there. As she read on she realized that Clint was quickly becoming a widely sought expert on the effects of off shore drilling on the environment. His research had been not only thorough, but unique. He'd had all kinds of contacts and delved into sources that most had no way of getting hold of. Articles about him said there was no stone he'd leave unturned. All well and good, but she needed more.

She decided to use Clint's password and log directly into his company's network .

There were letters from people turning to him for his opinion from all over the country, and beyond. Officials in Washington were contacting him regularly to support their bills. The information he gathered was vital to their decisions about where to drill, when and how. It seemed clear that Clint was doing a service to the entire world, both the drilling companies and the wild ocean life, shorelines, people, nations.

Fascinated, Cindy wanted to read the presentation he wrote that had been cancelled - his report on the Tearwall Project. It had to be somewhere here in his company files . Several other reports of his were there.

But to her surprise, the report on the Tearwall Project had been deleted.

Cindy sent out a flurry of emails to three or four people in the company then, asking if they had a copy.

It struck her then that the report might be on Clint's personal computer. She quickly went to it, logged in as him and checked. As she did, Cindy was surprised to see that Clint had been heavily downloading his files from work, the last few weeks before the wedding. The Tearwall

Project report had to be here. Cindy searched and searched.

It wasn't there .

She got up from the desk and stretched. It was after one in the morning. She'd completely lost her sense of time. But she couldn't sleep now, even if she wanted to. Her mind was spinning. She was troubled that Clint hadn't told her that his presentation had been cancelled. Why not? He must have been embarrassed by it. Or, was there something in it that he didn't want her to know? She couldn't discount that possibility. More and more aspects of Clint's life were now opening up in front of her eyes. She felt sick to her stomach. There was so much he hadn't shared.

As she looked about the room, the boxes of files along the back of the room caught her eye. Her heart leapt. Maybe there was a hard copy of the report stored there. He couldn't have just thrown it out. Cindy ran to the boxes and pulled them open.

These were neater, organized by subject and date, alphabetized in chronological order. That was a relief. She ruffled through them quickly. No sign or mention of The Tearwall Project Report.

Cindy put the packet of files down on her lap. Perspiration was running down her back. Where was that report? What happened to it? The report would contain both a copy of his presentation and details about the project itself. She absolutely had to have it. It couldn't have vanished into thin air.

She needed a break, but didn't have that luxury. Ann had been hurt. Who knew what would happen next? Both Heather and Clint's little son could be in danger. She thought of how Heather's face had grown ashen as she realized what was going on. Cindy didn't really know what had gone on between her and Clint, but she certainly couldn't let either of them be hurt. It wasn't fair.

What was fair? Cindy wondered, as she dwelt on everything. She remembered asking Clint about his research from time to time. He'd said by and large, it was confidential. She'd never probed further. She'd never probed anything. Those days were over now. There wasn't a sentence she'd now let go by.

Cindy had thought that Clint had told her everything about his life. They'd prided themselves on openness and honesty. Wrong. That frightened her. She'd always believed that life was fair, that there was order, balance and, at the end, justice for everyone. Now she questioned that .

It was disheartening going through his papers though, retracing his steps. But she needed specifics: names, dates, information. She'd have to contact the firm to get it.

Greg Hamden's name suddenly came to mind. He and Clint had worked so closely together on the project. Yes. He'd be able to fill in the gaps.

Then Cindy thought of Henry Greerson. Maybe he could also help. He'd called several times, saying he had something to give her. He'd asked to take her for coffee. Even though she never felt comfortable with him, Clint had always liked him. They'd worked closely together . Seemed like it was time to take him up now on his invitation.

Cindy got up, went to the window and looked out at the garden. It was the middle of the night. The trees were being wildly buffeted by the winds that had gone on all day without stopping. The house felt fragile in the storm; not really not able to hold up under the wind's constant onslaught. She was seized by a fear that a large branch would break off and crack the roof, or burst through the windows as the wind blew against the frail trees. Life suddenly seemed frail to Cindy, as though one could be blown away easily in any storm. She wondered what there was to hold onto? What could she really trust again?

It was almost morning, but Cindy still couldn't sleep. She needed to talk to Greg. Maybe he'd be willing to meet her for lunch?

Cindy sat back down at Clint's desk and emailed Greg, asking to set up a time for lunch.

To her surprise, an auto responder immediately replied.

Greg Hamden is no longer working for DGB Oil Company.

Cindy was shocked.

If you need to reach him, please contact his former assistant Bara, at the following phone number.

Cindy had no idea why Greg was no longer at the company. He'd been there even before Clint started working there.

She checked her watch: 5:15am. Bara wouldn't be in for a few more hours.

Eyes closing with exhaustion, Cindy decided to catch some sleep. And then to call Bara as soon as she woke.

*

Cindy woke at 9.15, and immediately called Bara. Clint's former assistant, Cindy knew her. They'd actually met a couple of times.

"I need to reach Greg Hamden," she said when Bara picked up the phone. "Can you let me know how to contact him?"

"I'm sorry, that information is not available," said Bara in a clipped tone.

This was ridiculous. Cindy would not be deterred. "It's extremely important."

"Who is this calling, please?"

"It's Cindy Blaine, Clint Blaine's wife." Cindy was reluctant to tell her, but had no choice.

There was a long silence on the other end of the phone, as if Cindy were the last person Bara expected to call.

"I'm so sorry about Clint," Bara said quietly then. "How are you?"

"I've been better," said Cindy.

"I'd love to help you, but -" Obviously, Bara had been told not to give any information out.

"Please," Cindy interrupted, "Greg was Clint's good friend. I don't think he knows what happened to him."

Bara stopped a moment. "That's right, Greg left before we heard about Clint."

"I know Clint would want him to be informed." Cindy was playing on her feelings blatantly, but she had no choice.

Bara relented. "Okay, don't tell anyone I'm giving you this." And she quickly gave Cindy Greg's phone number.

Cindy was thrilled to have it. "One more thing," Cindy continued quickly, "Do you happen to have a copy of Clint 's report on the Tearwall Project? The one he and Greg worked on?"

A stony silence greeted her.

"Are you there?" Cindy asked.

"Greg and Clint's business files were emptied out," Bara said. " I don't have any of them," Her voice became clipped again.

"There has to be a copy somewhere," Cindy said.

"You're pushing it," said Bara.

"Sorry," Cindy said, "and thanks for Greg's phone number."

Cindy hung up in amazement. Pushing what? The Tearwall Report was beginning to seem like the crowned jewels. What could be in it?

There were other people in the company who would know. Before Cindy contacted Greg, she sent a quick email to Greerson, telling him she'd love to arrange a time to meet.

*

Before she called Greg, Cindy went into the kitchen and poured a cup of steaming black coffee. Her lack of sleep the night before was beginning to take a toll. And Ann didn't look well. Not only was she still exhausted but had an odd pallor. Cindy couldn't let herself dwell on that now. But deep in the pit of her stomach, she was worried about her sister, scared that things weren't going well.

As soon as Cindy dialed his number, Greg picked up immediately.

"Who is it?" he said hurriedly.

"Greg, this is Cindy," she started, in an upbeat tone. She wanted to start out on the right foot. She'd met him in passing, a couple of times, and remembered him as a lively, positive guy.

"Cindy, who?" he sounded rushed.

"Cindy Blaine," she answered, disconcerted.

"Oh," he slowed down a second. "Well, congratulations on your marriage. How's Clint?"

Cindy felt a deep chill. "You haven't heard?"

"Heard what? I'm not working at the company anymore."

Cindy couldn't bring herself to say a thing.

"You didn't hear that I was let go?" Greg went on, even more hurriedly. "It happened while you guys were on your honeymoon. They told everyone I decided to leave. Well, it isn't true . Frankly, I was surprised that Clint didn't call when he got back to find out how I was . How come you're calling and he's not?" he seemed anxious to hang up.

Cindy didn't want to tell him over the phone. "I'd like to speak to you in person," she said. "Can we get together for lunch?"

"I'm not up to it," he said, scraping his throat. "Tell me what you have to now. I'm a busy man."

This was not the Greg that Cindy had known, the guy who used to be understanding.

"I can't talk about it over the phone," Cindy said.

That got him mad. "Listen, I've had enough talking about the company. I'm done with it. Over. There's nothing more I need to hear."

"Yes, there is," said Cindy softly.

"Listen, honey, I'm hanging up."

"Don't hang up," Cindy burst out, terrified of losing him. He was an important link to Clint. "Please, Greg, don't."

"What the hell is wrong?" he said bitterly. "Can't you respect my feelings? Just say what you have to over the phone."

"Clint is dead," Cindy announced bluntly.

Greg gasped.

"He was killed on our honeymoon."

"Oh my God."

"I need your help."

"Oh no, oh no," he couldn't speak.

"Please meet me in person. I need to talk to you."

Cindy thought she heard a sob. He was still for a few moments and then spoke in a raspy voice.

"You've got to be careful," he said fitfully. "We can't just meet anywhere."

"I'll meet you wherever you want."

"Go all the way over to the East River," he said in a hushed tone. "There's a Promenade near the river. It's pretty empty during the week. We can sit on a bench, around the bend."

The terror Greg felt poured through Cindy, making her heart clench.

"Okay," she said. She'd find out exactly where the Promenade was.

"I'll be there tomorrow at one o'clock," Greg continued furtively, "there's an entrance on 84th Street. Go East as far as you can. Then walk down to the river, and you'll be on the Promenade. Don't make a big deal of saying hello. Act as though everything's natural."

"Got it," said Cindy.

And then before she could say another word, she heard a dial tone.

Chapter 14

The next day was hot and humid. Cindy drove to the City with the car windows down, letting the warm, moist, sultry air wash over her. She parked on a side street, and walked a few blocks East to the Promenade. It was a lovely residential neighborhood, with brownstones on the side streets and tall, elegant apartment buildings on the main avenues. As she got further East she came to a neighborhood park which bordered the Promenade. There were trees, a playground, a basketball court. Then, beyond that, the walkway along the East River.

Cindy was almost afraid to walk down to the river. She had no idea what state Greg was in or what else she was going to find out.

A few ice cream vendors lined up along the entrance to the park, smiling at Cindy and asked if she wanted some. Cindy wished she could buy an ice cream for both her and Greg, but thought better of it. This meeting was peculiar. She didn't know how he would react.

She walked down the pathway slowly. When she got to the river, there he was, standing exactly where he said he would be .

Greg was a slim guy in his thirties, just a little taller than Cindy. He wore khaki pants, a blue tee shirt and a baseball cap, pulled low, with dark sunglasses. He saw her immediately, nodded and looked down.

Cindy came over stood next to him.

"Let's just walk," he said under his breath.

They started walking. As he'd said, the Promenade was mostly empty. A few people sat on benches at the river's edge, watching boats pass by. In the park that bordered the Promenade, some sunbathers were stretched out, lying on the grass. Thick, white summer clouds filled the sky.

Greg turned and looked over his shoulder a few times as they walked.

"We're going North," he told Cindy. "Right around that bend is a bench I love. It's under a big tree, protected from view."

"Great," Cindy said.

They came to the bend, turned a slight corner and there was a huge, sheltering tree. Under it was an empty bench.

"We'll sit here," Greg said instantly . "There's always a breeze."

Cindy and Greg sat down on the bench and he finally breathed a little more easily.

"They have tentacles everywhere," Greg said. "You have to be careful."

"Who has tentacles?" Cindy asked.

Greg turned and opened his huge brown eyes wide . "The company."

"I see," Cindy said.

"What do you see?" Greg was quick on the uptake. He was quick about everything, and right to the point.

"Not much," said Cindy.

"You're in danger."

It was as if a cold wind blew over Cindy. She'd felt there was danger, but to hear it said like that aloud made it more real, almost as if she could smell it. Otherwise, lulled by the beautiful trees, sky and late spring afternoon, the whole world seemed in harmony.

"Clint was never careful enough," Greg went on. "I told him that over and over."

Cindy couldn't let his fear overtake her.

"Clint loved to talk. He talked too much. He got so excited when he found something out, he'd tell everyone. I'd say, Clint, shut up. He called me paranoid. Oh God, I can't believe he's gone. He was a wonderful person."

Cindy wanted to put her hand on his quivering arm to comfort him, but he was too overwrought. He and Clint had worked together for three years. This had to be a huge shock.

"How'd he die?" he finally asked.

"The Coroner called it accidental drowning."

"Bullshit," Greg blurted out. "Did you see the Coroner's report yourself?"

"No. I wasn't in shape to see anything then."

"Check the Coroner's report yourself," Greg said.

She would. That was a good idea.

"Why did they fire you, Greg?"

"I'll tell you what I can. I'm only here because of Clint. I have an agreement with the company not to say anything to anyone. That's not unusual in a termination agreement. In exchange they gave me some funds."

"I'm not just anyone."

"I'm not stupid. I realize that. And I have a moral obligation to keep you from harm. Clint's death was definitely not an accident."

Cindy was beginning to feel cold and edgy.

"Clint went much too far. He got a lot of warnings to stop poking around in the research he was doing. "

"Research on the Tearwall Project?"

"He wasn't supposed to tell you about it."

"He didn't. I found out."

"He always had to go to the limit with everything. But the company had millions and millions of dollars committed to the drill. The more we explored, the worse it looked. You get the drift of what I'm saying? He was digging up information nobody wanted. "

"I need dates, facts to bring to the authorities," Cindy said.

Greg turned and looked at her straight on. "There are lobbyists involved. Congressmen. You think the cops can help?"

"I need facts, details," said Cindy.

"Whew. You're just like him. Playing with fire."

Greg looked out at the river that stretched before them. "Beautiful here, isn't it?" he said.

"Very," said Cindy.

"Peaceful, secluded." Greg tapped his fingers along the bench. "If you're quiet, you can even hear the birds singing in these trees."

"He didn't believe it when I told him he was putting us in danger."

"Why not?" Cindy zeroed in.

"Clint discovered something too big to handle. But he wouldn't let up. He was like a dog with a bone, felt he was out there, saving the world."

With that, Greg was done. He got up from the bench abruptly. "Who did he save? Not even himself." He looked very sad then.

"Wait a minute," Cindy reached out for him. "Please, I need more information to go to the police."

"It's bigger than that. They won't be able to do anything for you. They take orders from above."

"Then I'll go to the police."

"Keep dreaming," Greg said. "The best thing you can do now is get out of town . Don't threaten the company. Don't poke around. Pretend Clint's death was an accident. Play the part of the grieving widow."

"Forget it," she said. "How could I live with myself if I kept everything buried? What do you think of me?" Cindy felt worse than before.

"At least you'd live," Greg smiled oddly.

"I'm begging you, I need more information."

"And I need to stay alive," said Greg.

Then he suddenly turned, waved, and quickly rushed away, and disappeared, around another bend.

Cindy was left standing there alone, under the tree. She wondered exactly what Clint had discovered. It had cost him his life. Now Greg was running for his as well.

Cindy looked up at the beautiful, sheltering tree and realized that her life wasn't worth anything, if it wasn't based on the truth. She had no intention of running away from this. She'd get the help she needed somehow.

Chapter 15

Greerson was thrilled to hear from Cindy when she called.

"Meet me at five tonight, at the St. Regis lobby. There's a lovely spot for coffee there."

The lobby of the St. Regis was a wonderful place to collect herself. Cindy got there half an hour earlier and sat down on the plush red velvet sofas, waiting for Greerson to appear. Everything in the hotel was in perfect order, guests dressed elegantly, hotel attendants solicitous about one's every need. There was a large, round, gold clock over the registration desk. Sitting here it seemed as if nothing untoward could ever happen, that all were taken care of.

Greerson entered dressed in a pin-striped suit. He was well dressed, prepared as usual. He greeted her warmly, and led her to the cafe behind the lobby. It was a perfect spot for coffee. Greerson ordered his coffee black.

"How are you, Cindy?" he put his hand on hers.

"Doing better," she said and smiled. She felt comforted for a moment. For a moment she wondered why she had never liked him. Just passing feelings that meant nothing, she thought.

"We have a little gift for you," Greerson said then, taking Cindy by surprise . "There's a policy in the company that when there is a death of an employee, we offer the spouse a grievance check to help them get back on their feet. In honor of Clint and how much he meant to us, let us present this to you."

He handed the envelope to Cindy. "I'm sure it will be a while before the insurance kicks in and everything else is taken care of. This will hold you nicely until then. You won't have to worry, and can settle back into your life."

Cindy looked at it. Ten thousand dollars. What was this, some kind of bribe? Some kind of payoff, to keep her silent? Was that was Clint's life was worth? Ten thousand dollars?

Cindy let it sit on the table for now.

The waiter poured both of them cups of steaming coffee.

"So, tell me how your days are going?" Greerson said, lifting the cup to his mouth.

"Busy going through Clint's files," she said, "trying to understand everything."

Greerson put the cup down. He didn't like it. "What is there to understand?"

"All kinds of things," said Cindy.

He paused, looking disconcerted. He cleared his throat.

"I hear that you're sending emails to people in the company asking about this and that, as well."

"I'm looking for answers," she said bluntly, "about why Clint died."

He picked up his cup, drained it. "Still with that? "

"It wasn't a natural death."

"You should be out unwinding, getting a massage, talking to friends, going back to your job."

It struck Cindy that Greerson thought that by accepting the check, she would go along with the company's plans and wishes, forget about probing further .

Greerson leaned forward, "Actually," he said, "We have questions as well. We'd like to review some of Clint's files ourselves. There are reports he was working on that we need now. Letters, documents, things like that. I'm sure you understand."

Cindy understood better than he could ever know. They wanted his files. They probably searched for them and realized Clint had taken them off the company computer before he died. They must have thought he had hard copies stored at the house as well.

There was no way she was going to give them to him . "I'll have to check with my lawyer," she said.

"What lawyer?" Greerson looked surprised.

"My personal lawyer," Cindy said lightly.

"Clint's business files have nothing to do with you," Greerson's voice grew steely. "Actually, they're company property. Clint worked on them while he was in our employ."

Cindy smiled, "I'll just have to check." She was buying time.

Greerson's face became drawn. "Are you going to make this hard for us Cindy? We don't take well to playing games."

It was clearly a warning. "I'm not playing games," she said, "I'm just going step by step."

Greerson reached out then and touched Cindy's arm kindly. "I know this all must be overwhelming for you," he said. "Why don't you give us the name of your lawyer and we'll work it out with him."

Cindy blanched. There was no lawyer.

"Let me think about it," Cindy said.

"What exactly is there to think about?" Greerson said, his eyes narrowing.

Cindy felt intimidated. He was setting up a deal for her, as he had done with Greg. But she wasn't buying it. She had no intention of doing what Greerson wanted. Maybe the company did own Clint's files, but she had a right to know what was in them first . It was her husband that had lost his life. She couldn't let it all be for nothing.

Greerson looked at the envelope laying on the table. "There's something you're forgetting," he said, sliding the envelope towards her.

She looked at it, then slid it back.

"That's blood money," she said coldly. "You can keep it."

Greerson stared back at her, his eyes turning to ice.

He grabbed the envelope, got up swiftly, smoothed his suit, and without another word, turned and left.

Chapter 16

Cindy realized that whatever was in Clint's files must be important, if Greerson was so eager to have it. She realized that she had to track it down. That it might just be the key to exactly what he was up to, to exactly why they'd wanted Clint killed.

But as she stood there, in his office, she realized she'd looked everywhere—combed his entire place up and down. She scanned the desk, the drawers, the file cabinets, the boxes…she couldn't imagine where else could it be.

Where would Clint hide something valuable? she asked herself.

Then she realized. His safe.

She crossed the room, removed the painting from the wall, and stared at the metal safe. It could only be opened with the key. And suddenly, with a pang, she remembered where the key was.

Clint's mother's basement. His favorite place to store things he deemed too valuable to keep lying around the house.

His mom would never let Cindy into her basement. Cindy wouldn't even bother calling.

Cindy thought. She remembered that the basement in Clint's mom's home had a small side window that let in some light. Clint had once mentioned casually that the window was usually unlocked. Cindy could go there, push it open and crawl down inside. There were only three or four boxes of Clint's files left there. She knew the key to his safe had to be in one of them . She remembered him saying he was putting it there.

It would be best to go later, when it was dark. Then nobody would see her in the yard, crawling in. Clint's mom and dad upstairs would probably be sleeping or watching TV, and would never hear any noise downstairs. Cindy could jog all the way there, and no one would hear a car pull up or see her slip down through the window into the basement.

Cindy went back into Clint's study to wait until it got dark out. It was familiar and comforting to be there now. She sat down on the old, navy shag rug, and ran her hand over it. So many times she and Clint sat on it together, holding hands. She wondered if he had any idea of what was going on in this world? If he missed it? Or, was he happy where he was?

Finally, it was almost dark out. Time to go.

As she jogged to Clint's mother's house, she could almost feel him jogging beside her in the misty, summer rain, urging her on. Once at the house, she moved swiftly on the soft, damp grass, under the blanket of darkness that had fallen.

Cindy went to the side basement window, bent down and pushed hard . It opened right away.

Cindy curled up, put her head in first, squirmed back and forth and slid the rest of her body in through the window. Holding onto the side of the wall, it was easy to lower the rest of her body down into the basement. So far all was going easily. Only a few steps left to get the key. Why did Clint's family have to make everything so hard? She was doing this for them, too.

It was dark down in the basement, but Cindy remembered that the boxes were over against the far wall. She quickly made her way over. There were four of them there. In the dim light that came from the open window, she could barely make out what was in each of them. Two of them were opened. Whoever had opened them hadn't even bothered to put back the tops. It had to be Ralph, looking for personal information. He wouldn't have had any interest in Clint's business files. That's where Clint had said he'd put the key. Cindy dragged those boxes closer to the open window to get some light. Once there, she pulled off the tops.

The first box was filled with papers, filed carefully. No key.

She opened the second box. In the back of it she saw a sealed envelope. Cindy ripped it open.

There it was. She held up the key and stared at it. Then she slipped it into her pocket. This was the prize. There was no doubt about it.

Cindy knew she should get out of there immediately, but, unable to contain her curiosity, she decided to rummage through the second box. Who knew what else Clint had buried in them? Time passed as she sat there, engrossed, reading his older presentations, and she didn't hear the footsteps that came down the stairs.

Lights flashed on suddenly, shocking her. She screamed.

"Who the hell is down here?" a rough voice boomed.

Cindy jumped, terrified.

"Don't make a move," a person came closer.

Cindy looked over. It was Ralph. She was both relieved and distraught.

"What the hell are you doing here?" he came right over, up close, to her.

"I needed to get something that belonged to Clint," she answered swiftly.

"Like hell. You're looking for the money."

"Look," she motioned to the boxes," they're his business files."

"You think I was born yesterday, Cindy?" His face was flushed and his mouth drawn tight. Cindy had never seen him like this before. "How did you even get down here? Who said you could come in?"

"Those boxes are Clint's property," Cindy stepped back a few feet. He was too close, breathing heavily on her.

"You got a lawyer? He told you to do this? Breaking and entering?"

For a quick moment Ralph seemed consumed, insane.

"I'm trying to find out who murdered Clint," Cindy said. "I don't care about your money."

Ralph guffawed. "Who killed him?" He was mocking her, "You probably killed him for the insurance yourself. I got it figured out. You put something in his food, so when he went surfing, he wouldn't be able to handle the waves. Then the insurance would be all yours. Now you're trying to find the killer. Very smart, blaming it on someone else."

Ralph was paranoid and terrifying, There was no reasoning with him .

"You know we tried to stop this marriage before it even took place," he went on. "Clint wouldn't listen. Damn guy was headstrong, and it cost him his life."

"Who exactly tried to stop it?" Cindy was on the alert. "You and who else?"

"Clint's best man, Al."

Cindy was shocked.

"He took Clint out of town and talked to him about it all day long. He never liked you. He didn't like that Clint was tying the knot in only a year. All Clint could say, over and over, was that he'd never let you go. Nobody understood why."

Hot, stinging tears filled Cindy's eyes. That explained his day in Boston with Al.

"I loved him, too," she said, filled with pain. "I never would hurt him in anyway."

Ralph sneered. "You loved him, huh? Did you know Al had a photo of one of Clint's girls. The two of them had a kid together."

Cindy felt devastated . "How did he know?"

"He saw the kid. He told me. He's a dead ringer for Clint."

Cindy breathed a little easier. That explained it.

"Clint didn't know the first thing about the kid, for a long time," Ralph went on. "But at the end, before the wedding, he knew. Al sent the photo to him. It was a last ditch effort to wake him up."

Ralph didn't know that Clint never received the photo in the mail.

He laughed. "I bet he didn't tell you a thing about it?"

There wasn't any length they'd go to, to rip her and Clint apart. Even after he was gone. But it wouldn't work.

"He never got the photo, Ralph."

Ralph coughed.

"I found it. After he died."

"Well, he was damn stupid. And don't think that woman isn't going to come and claim insurance money for the kid as soon as she finds out. All you women - ."

All of a sudden he grinned. He had tiny teeth all crunched together. "Finding you down here like this, proves my theory," he said. "Why in hell would anyone crawl down into the basement, if they weren't out to fleece us? But whether you know it or not, we've got the Will and insurance policy. The insurance wasn't signed right - and honey, there's no mention of you in the will. He never bothered to change a word of the Will after he met you."

Why would he, Cindy thought? They were young and healthy . And as for the insurance policy, she'd get a lawyer to straighten things out. And she'd be happy to give a nice chunk of it to Clint's son. For now, she only wanted to get out of there.

But Ralph had other ideas. He closed in.

"Clint's dad is coming to the end," he said. "Marge knows it. There's a lot of money that's going to be passed around."

He was too close, breathing in Cindy's face again. Then he rubbed her shoulders with his hands.. She tried to shake him off, but he only came closer.

"I always thought you were a pretty lady," he said, "much prettier than Marge." Cindy felt like throwing up.

"Get away from me," she said, and twisted her shoulders to get free of him . She couldn't.

He pressed them tighter, pulled her to him and pushed himself up against her. Sick to her stomach, she struggled to toss him off her. She couldn't.

He reached up for her face. She spun it to the other side. God knows what he was planning to do.

"Are you crazy?" she breathed. "I'll have you locked up."

He guffawed again. "By who?"

His wet mouth was all over neck.

"I know every move you make." Then he pulled at her face, so he could kiss her. She yanked her head the other way.

"You're sick," Cindy breathed, "When I tell Marge -"

He grabbed her tighter. "Honey, you tell Marge about this, and you're as good as finished."

Cindy was enraged. She felt a surge of strength she never knew she had, and with all her power took both her hands and shoved him away. Taken by surprise, he tipped backwards and slid on the floor.

In that precious second, Cindy flew upstairs, through the open front door, and ran into the night like a criminal, speeding away. Ralph was a monster. She never wanted to lay eyes on him again. But, at least she had the key. All the rest was garbage.

*

Cindy flew home and went straight to Clint's study. The run home had been fast and furious and her body was shaking.

She ran to Clint's study, pulled out the key, put it into his safe's lock, and turned it. The safe opened instantly.

Chapter 17

Cindy had expected to see the safe packed with papers, valuables.

But to her surprise, it was nearly empty. There was only one, tiny thing sitting inside it: a thumb drive.

She held it up and stared at it, wondering what could be on it. Then she hurried over and inserted it into his computer.

Up came a message. Directory access was locked . Password protected.

God, help, please, she cried out . Cindy was so muddled and exhausted, she couldn't remember what some of his passwords might be.

She tried entering a few that she knew Clint used regularly. Neither of them opened the file.

She switched around some letters and tried again.

None worked.

You've got to help me, Clint, she thought.

Her head cleared a little. Then, from nowhere, it struck her to try her name.

She typed in *Cindy*.

To her amazement, the directory opened.

Thank you, Clint, she thought. *Thank you.*

She quickly scanned the contents. —It was there. The Tearwall Project Report. A huge burst of energy came over her. Cindy immediately opened it and started reading,

First she found a general report about offshore drilling that went on for pages. It was titled: Ecological Zones in Offshore Drilling. It detailed the harm expected by drilling in the wrong area. Attached to the report was responses by others.

What, then, is the true value of an oil well drilled a mile down offshore in a unique ecological zone subject to multiple uses? Is it simply the cost of the well or the price of the product? For example, let's look carefully at the Tearwall Project. What are the ancillary expenses, revenues and losses and the consequences of possible disaster? Much too large for comfort. Much too much risk for the public versus what can be gained.

A response from someone said, "Let's drop this right now, Clint."

Obviously he hadn't. Cindy read on.

And let's not forget the environmental refugees, the communities affected, the damage to the productive ecology. From a balance sheet perspective, what in the near term seems like profit is in the long term a financial disaster. We saw this just a few months ago in the photos of oil slicks, wide and deep. We saw fouled beaches, dead wildlife, destroyed wetlands, unemployed fishermen, bankrupt tourism businesses, depressed local economies, ruined communities.

A response from a man named Lew Dorin, at the firm, was attached. It said, *Clint. A big decision is coming down in Washington. We need to let the bill pass.*

Beneath that was another letter, from Henry Greerson.

Fine report, Clint. We'll keep it on hold for the next month or six weeks. Expecting a sizable government allocation. Once that's in, we'll deal with these facts and assess the way we wish to proceed.

Under that was a letter from Greerson's assistant.

The consequences of drilling there are enormous, dangerous. We're looking at more than earthquakes, it's massive human, animal and ecological devastation.

Obviously, Clint's company, DGB, had been commissioned to do a massive drilling project. They were just ready to start. A few months before the project was to begin, there was trouble in Washington regarding it.

Clint had included all kinds of reports backing up his conclusions. There was a report on an explosion that left eleven dead and slathered Alabama's beaches due to an oil spill.

There was big money here and big promises. The government was involved on many fronts. Clint's reports could potentially affect millions of dollars and millions of lives.

There was a note attached to that report signed by Greerson.

Great research Clint. Let's file this report for future reference. Take a break from research dealing with spills and faults.

Clint hadn't gone along. Seemed like he continued unearthing more information. Immediately after that, he wrote and sent out another report.

Cindy looked carefully at the responses to his reports from people at the firm. In the beginning they were complimentary, commenting on his attention to detail and thoroughness. As time went on, there were more and more letters telling him to stop. Drop it. His reports were becoming hot potatoes.

Clint paid no attention, just continued on. They hadn't been able to stop him.

Or had they?

It seemed obvious what had happened. Clint had pushed it too far. And they had gotten rid of him. They waited for a time and place that was convenient, a place, like Barbados, like the rough surf of the ocean, where it wouldn't be clear it was a murder, where suspicions would not be raised. It was all too much for Cindy to bear.

She had to make sense of it all. She needed confirmation, needed to know that she wasn't crazy.

Then it came to her. Greg. He would know. He would know for sure. She had to share this report with him, had to hear his opinion of it. What exactly were its consequences?

Cindy picked up her phone and dialed Greg. It rang for a long while. Finally, someone picked up.

"Hello," a female voice answered.

"I'm sorry to be calling so late," Cindy said, "just wanted to talk to Greg."

Silence on the other end.

"Is he there?" said Cindy.

"No," the voice sounded distant and odd.

"Can I call later tonight? Is tomorrow better?"

"Tomorrow isn't better," the voice sounded devastated.

"Is something wrong?" Cindy's heart leapt.

"Greg died suddenly of heart failure, yesterday," she said.

Cindy gasped. "Who's this?"

"His sister. We knew he had a weak heart, but no one expected him to die. It wasn't that bad. He was so young. It happened out of the blue."

Cindy was silent.

"At least he didn't suffer," she said.

Cindy wondered what really happened.

"We'll have a memorial later on," said his sister. "He wanted to be cremated. Call in a week and I'll let you know."

Cindy was utterly, completely speechless. Her stomach started hurting badly, and she doubled over with cramps. Was Greg's death her fault too? Had the company been watching him and seen him speaking to her? Would this have happened if she'd never called?

This was the third person that had been killed or hurt around Cindy. For a moment she wanted to let it all go, call a truce, go back to the company, take the check and give it all to Heather for Clint's son.

Cindy lay down on the couch exhausted and shattered . The company was bigger than her, richer, stronger. It had ammunition she couldn't even imagine. But she had something better on her side. Justice. She thought of the little Bible Tom Mallord had given her. Words from it flashed through her mind.

Whatever you do for the least of my creatures, you do for me.

Someone had to stand up for fairness and compassion. Otherwise, what was it all worth?

She would not back down, not be afraid any longer. She needed a voice of reason, a clear direction. She thought of Ann. Yes. Ann would know exactly what to do.

Chapter 18

Ann was laying in the hospital bed with her eyes closed when Cindy walked into the room. She'd developed a low grade fever and her recovery was slower than expected. The nurse told her that Frank had flown home for the night and would be back for the weekend. Ann opened her eyes, pleased to see Cindy, but then shut them again. She still looked exhausted.

Cindy put the fruit and cookies she'd brought on a table near the bed, sat down next to her sister and took her hand.

"Slow going?" asked Cindy.

"I'm getting there," Ann managed to reply.

"The doctors say you're doing well," Cindy said, trying to be encouraging. "Once the fever goes, you'll be ready for physical therapy. They might even discharge you in a few days."

Ann nodded.

"These things take time," Cindy said.

"Everything takes time," Ann whispered. "Time is good."

Cindy wondered how Ann could say that, laying here in pain.

"I'm so sorry, Ann," Cindy said again.

Ann shook her head, as she always did when Cindy said that. She meant there was nothing to be sorry about.

"The report about the brakes came back from the police," Cindy said quietly, to fill up the empty time. "They were definitely tampered with."

Ann shook her head, back and forth again, trying to same something.

"What is it?" Cindy asked.

Ann lifted herself, came closer. "You were right all along," she said.

Cindy didn't know what she meant. Then she suddenly got it. "Right about Clint?"

Ann fell back down on the pillow and nodded.

Cindy's heart swelled to hear that, to hear that.

Finally, she believed her, didn't think she was crazy. She felt encourage to go on.

"Ann," Cindy began, "I found a lot of troubling information. About Clint's company. I have a report he wrote...I know it sound crazy, but I think he was getting ready to implicate them. And I think they got rid of him."

Ann nodded.

"And I think that whoever got rid of him wants me dead, too."

"Do you any proof?" Ann asked.

"Just one report he wrote. But it's pretty damning."

Ann nodded, eyes drifting in and out.

"What should I do?" Cindy asked. "Go to the police."

Ann shook her head.

"The FBI," Ann said.

Cindy's eyes opened wide.

"It's an international crime," Ann continued. "You need the FBI. Go. Don't wait."

Ann's words gave Cindy a chill. They also gave her courage, determination to go on. She squeezed her hand as her eyes drifted closed and she knew, once again, that Ann was right.

Chapter 19

Cindy's meeting with Officer James E. Farnell at the FBI took less than fifteen minutes. Farnell was a big, heavy set, square jawed guy, who'd been through this a thousand times. Cindy brought all the information she had about Clint's death, along with everything that had happened since then, including the company reports, and placed it all squarely on Farnell's desk.

He sat there chewing on his bottom lip, examining the papers.

His eyes half closed, he peered at Cindy. "It's all circumstantial," he finally said.

Cindy'd heart dropped. "You won't take on the case?" she asked.

"There's no case here," he said.

Cindy's heart dropped.

"I'm not saying it's not adding up. It's interesting," Farnell stuck out his jaw and tapped his thumb on it. "I need more. Something solid, something direct. You're asking us to take on an international oil drilling firm, with connections in Washington. This isn't enough."

"Help me out," Cindy said suddenly aggrieved.

"Sorry," Farnell said.

"Wait a minute," Cindy got angry. "You're telling me to just forget it?"

A little smile crept around the edges of her mouth. He liked her spunk. Cindy saw that.

"No, I'm not. I'm saying there's not enough here to start an investigation."

"What else do I need?"

"Get me the original Coroner's report," Farnell said. "I want to see it firsthand. Get me a witness. Who found the body? Who collected evidence? What did they find? And what about the crime scene?"

Cindy's mind was racing. She pulled out her pad and started taking notes.

"The crime scene was in the ocean," she said, tears suddenly filling her eyes.

"How do you know?"

That stopped Cindy cold.

"What kind of evidence was collected? I need the exact condition of the body, what exactly was inside it or outside?

"I'd have to go back to Barbados to get those kinds of specifics," she breathed.

"So, go," he said.

The second he said it, a jolt raced through Cindy. She knew it was right. It felt right. Yes. Barbados. Of course. She had to go back.

Cindy felt nervous, but excited.

"Can I keep in touch with you?"

"Send me evidence if you get it, and I'll take a look.

And as far as all of your theories about DGB and the sudden death of Greg…"

"Hamden," Cindy said.

He wrote it down. "Hamden, right…well, I'm not promising anything, but I'll look into it," he relented.

"I don't know how to thank you," Cindy said.

"Don't thank me yet," he said. "Let's see what you come up."

Cindy stood.

"One more thing," he added.

She stopped and turned.

"If there was some sort of cover up down there, you might be walking into the hornet's nest. If the local police were paid off, if they had a hand in falsifying evidence, then don't go looking to them for help."

Cindy swallowed, nervous. She hadn't thought of that.

"But then…" she began, "who can I turn to?"

"Just keep your head low, get what you need, and come back," he said. "But if you find yourself in any kind of trouble, get to the U.S. Embassy. And call me from there."

Cindy's heart pounded in her chest, as she wondered how badly all of this could go.

Chapter 20

Cindy raced home in Clint's car, anxious to pack her things and catch the next plane she could to Barbados. The FBI agent was right: she'd never get the answers she really wanted unless she went back there. And no one else was going to do it for her. If she really wanted to solve this, to honor Clint's life, if she really wanted to put this all to rest, she'd just have to go back.

The more she thought about it, The more she realized that this would also give her a chance to go back to where she and Clint had been so happy. She realized that a part of her had been longing for this—to be back in the place where they were happy, to be able to pick up where they'd left off.

She'd book a room in the same hotel, talk to the staff, see the Coroner, find out the exact condition of Clint's body. All things she hadn't been able to do before. She would go to the beach where he had gone surfing and tell him herself.

Cindy pulled into the driveway, anxious to get rolling and check the available flights.

Excited, she ran to the door, opened it up and walked into the house.

A cold wave of fear gripped her.

The place was turned upside down. Tables were knocked over, a curtain torn, magazines scattered on the floor, her favorite vase smashed . Someone had broken in.

She ran into Clint's study. All his files were gone - along with his computer.

Thank God she still had the thumb drive, and had left hard copies safe with the FBI.

She ran into the bedroom to see if her computer was gone too. She'd taken to keeping it under the bed, so she could reach for it in the middle of the night. Miraculously, it was still there.

Cindy immediately reached for the phone and called Officer Fenlen. To her great relief, he picked up.

"Someone broke into my house," she told him immediately. "They grabbed all the files."

Fenlen was quiet.

"I'm scared."

"Call the local police. File a report. And get yourself to Barbados. I'll inform the U.S. consulate that you're coming. Stay in close touch."

Chapter 21

Cindy booked the first flight that was available, a late night flight that was half empty, and leaving that very night.

When she got to the airport, she felt as though she were going back in time. She and Clint had also taken a late night flight, that left right after the wedding.

"It went great, it went great," he kept saying, his arms around her, kissing her.

"I never thought we'd have such a wonderful time. And our families were also happy. My father and your mother talked a long time. The band was better than I ever thought it would be. And did you see Al dancing?"

Cindy had smiled and smiled. She was exhausted but completely content. She now had all that she had ever wanted. She couldn't wait to get to the beach and lay together on the sand, away from everyone.

As they'd boarded the plane, Clint kept talking and laughing. He was probably a little high, she'd thought, from all the champagne.

"Do you have any idea how much I love you?" he kept whispering in Cindy's ear, over and over during the flight. It was as though he'd climbed Mt. Everest and finally reached the top.

Cindy wasn't sure why he loved her so much, but was happy to hear it, able for the first time in her life, to take it in. She was sure they had a lifetime of trips like this ahead of them.

Now she slept alone on the plane most of the way. It felt good being in the air, leaving the mess in the city behind. But she was also nervous about what lay ahead of her.

As the plane flew through the air, she dreamt of Clint. She dreamt that they were on their honeymoon, drinking champagne. They were back at the hotel, with soft ocean breezes soothing them. Then, out of the corner of her eye, Cindy saw a small, pocked marked man, carrying a tray with food for them. The tray was made out of the skin of dead snakes. Cindy shuddered and let out a little scream. The man dropped the tray and started running over the rocks, out to the shore, as the snakes slithered wildly all over the floor.

Cindy awoke suddenly on the plane and reached out for Clint's hand, thinking they were still together. But the seat next to her was empty. She shook her head, turned and looked, and then fell back into a restless sleep.

"Prepare for landing," Cindy was awakened by the sound of the stewardess voice over the loudspeaker. "We will be descending in about fifteen minutes. "

Cindy couldn't believe they were about to land. She sat up and began to gather her things. Through the plane window she could see the early morning light begin to rise. A new day.

She closed her eyes and breathed deeply. She had no idea how much she'd wanted to be back here. She felt so close to Clint, returning to Barbados, as though nothing had changed, as though the world was stable and filled with joy.

The landing was smooth, and as the plane was half empty it took no time getting off. Cindy went down a shaky plank, got a cup of coffee to take with her at a nearby stand, and walked to the luggage rack to wait for her baggage.

Soon the turnstile began to spill out the few pieces the plane had carried. Cindy watched the passengers pick up their luggage in the still sleepy airport. Hers came last. She took it and went outside to get a cab.

As she walked to the taxi line, the warm, salty air washed over her, relaxing her muscles and bringing a smile to her face. With all that had happened, it was still wonderful being here. Cindy shook her hair out and let it fall loosely to her shoulders as she looked up at the sky. It was soft blue, with light clouds drifting playfully overhead. She felt so at home here in the

Caribbean, as if this were exactly where she belonged.

As she waited a few moments for a cab, she wondered if she would get the same driver she and Clint had before.

She didn't. A tall, thin young man, drove up. He got out of the cab, put her luggage in the back as she got in.

"El Barado Hotel," she said.

Just as the driver on their honeymoon, this one stopped, turned around and looked at her oddly. "You sure?"

"Very sure."

"You know where you're going?"

Cindy wondered if all the drivers were instructed to warn travelers before taking them there.

"Most go to the West Coast," He said. "There's plenty of rooms available there."

"I always go to the El Barado," said Cindy.

"Always? Yeah? You like it there?"

Cindy didn't feel like having a discussion, She wanted to get to the hotel.

"Let's go," she said.

He made a face, turned around, started the car, turned on the radio loud, and drove off.

"Can you make the radio lower?" she said.

"I like it loud," he said.

The radio blared reggae music for most of the drive. Cindy leaned near the window and looked out at the little villages she and Clint had passed. Rows of sugar cane farms and tiny villages of single-story houses once again dotted the landscape. It was early, nothing had woken up yet and the villages seemed eerie, almost ghost towns, with barely one person to be seen.

In what seemed like no time, the cab wound up the narrow road, behind bushes and towering palm trees, to the El Barado hotel, nestled in the rocks, besides the ocean. And the beach that had claimed Clint's life.

Everything seemed closed. The cab parked in front of the hotel and to Cindy's surprise the driver tooted his horn loudly to let them know they'd arrived. Then he got out to get her luggage.

Cindy got out of the cab. It was shocking to be back here. The place was exactly as she remembered it, with nothing changed, except that the clouds were quickly becoming a little heavier, and the wind was picking up.

The driver went back into the cab and leaned on his horn again.

"It's nothing, miss," he said grinning. "Do it all the time. Got to let them know they got a guest."

At that very second, the entrance door to the hotel flung open and Alex came running out, his arms spread wide.

"Miss Cindy, Miss Cindy" he said, moved to see her. "What a pleasure to have you back here with us."

Cindy was thrilled to see him. But it also felt odd, arriving so early and alone. This was a honeymoon spot for couples. But Alex knew she'd been here with Clint. He remembered what had happened, had taken a special interest in them. She hadn't gotten to say good-bye to him properly when she'd left before. That last day was all a blur. They'd put her on sedatives to calm her down. Greerson had been there, accompanying her to the airport. She didn't remember seeing Alex at all at the end.

Cindy ran up to him now. He was such a strong connection to Clint. She wanted to hug him, like an old friend, but stopped just a moment before she did.

He held out both hands and grasped hers in them.

"I'm so sorry," he said, his eyes welling up with tears.

Cindy grasped his hands in hers. They gave her strength and comfort.

"Your room is ready," Alex said.

She'd reserved the same room she and Clint had stayed in.

"I thought maybe you'd like another room," Alex said tentatively then. "If you want to change rooms, you can."

"No," Cindy said. She wanted to go through all the steps exactly as they happened. "No, I appreciate it. I want the room we stayed in before."

Alex took the baggage from the cab driver, who was listening intently to every word. Cindy paid, tipped and thanked him. He took the money, grinned at her and left slowly through the front door. Cindy was glad he was gone.

Alex picked up her luggage. "Did you have a good trip?" he asked,

"Perfect, easy," said Cindy.

Alex smiled. "Very good, very good. Let's go get you settled. "

She followed him upstairs to the room. He opened it and the two of them walked inside.

The room was exactly as she remembered it, the patio overlooking the wide expanse of teeming ocean, the wooden shutters flapped lightly against the windows. Cindy took a deep, salty breath. The huge king bed they'd slept in was there, and so were the seashells and conches, laid out in straw baskets on the table.

Alex put her baggage down and seemed to want to say something, but fought it back, staying silent. He probably wanted to say how sorry he was. He was probably also wondering what in the world she was doing back here now. She would tell him, in good time . Now, she took out some bills to thank Alex.

He shook his head. "Not necessary, Miss. It's a pleasure to have you here." Then he turned to leave and stopped at the door. "I hope your stay will be pleasant. If I can help you with anything, Miss Cindy, I'm right here."

And then he left.

Cindy was relieved to be alone in the room. She went to the bed and ran her hand over the light blue, cotton bedspread, the same one that had been here before. She pulled the bedspread off the bed and held it close, as if she were wrapping Clint around her.

Cindy lay down and stretched out on the bed, looking up at the high wooden, ceiling. She listened to the wind in the palm trees outside and breathed the salt air . Everything was exactly the same as before.

Laying there, she felt Clint's spirit with her strongly. She hadn't felt it so powerfully before and felt certain that he would guide her every step of the way.

As she lay there, Cindy went over all the things she wanted to do that day.

First she wanted to walk on the beach, retrace where it happened.

Then, she would go straight to the Coroner's office to get the report. She needed details about the condition of Clint's body. Up to now she hadn't been able to bear even thinking about that. But here in Barbados, a strong energy filled her. She felt planted in nature, powerful and able to deal with anything.

Cindy closed her eyes and slept for a little while and then awoke, swiftly, upset with herself. She hadn't meant to take a nap. The trip must have tired her out more than she thought.

She checked her watch and jumped out of bed and headed right down to the beach.

Even this early in the day, the tides were in and the waves rolling roughly onto shore. Cindy loved the sound of the pounding turf. It cleared her mind and helped her see details she'd never seen before. She and Clint had run along this very beach together. It felt wonderful being here now. She ran faster and faster, in tune to the beat of the waves.

She stopped at the stretch of beach where she'd gone that day Clint died, the spot where his surfboard floated up. It had been a day pretty much like this one, only the surf had been calmer. Cindy stood there looking out at the ocean and gazing around on the beach. There was nothing there that said that a man's life had been cut short at this spot. That the surf had swallowed him up. As if nothing had happened, the waves simply rolled on.

Farnell's questions came to mind. How did she know Clint died at this spot? His surfboard had floated up here, but that didn't prove anything . It was a waste of time to stand here wondering. She had to get to the Coroner's office, see the report for herself, get the facts.

Cindy broke into a run back. As she ran, she realized how much of this amazing life she'd been blind to. She'd lived in a tiny corner of the world with familiar people and situations. There was no way she could go back to living like that.

It was time to open her eyes and go deeper into the island and what it had done to the man she'd loved.

*

Cindy rented a car and drove herself to the Coroner's office in town. It took a little while to get used to driving here, on the left side of the road.

It was about a two mile drive along a winding road. The Coroner's office was a three story building in the Center of town, surrounded by some other small buildings, painted white.

Cindy parked and got out.

Little pebbles were scattered along the main pathway and toads scampered here and there. Cindy entered the building and asked a man who sat on a stool where the Coroner's office was. He barely took notice of her, just pointed straight down the hall. "Wait a few minutes. The secretary's on a break . Wait over there and I'll call you when she comes back."

He motioned to a small waiting alcove with wooden benches.

Cindy went over and sat down. There was a rickety grandfather's clock standing in it and little tables near the benches with brochures about Barbados and all kinds of articles. There was also a big fan in the corner, whirring, cooling those who came here to wait. Cindy picked up one of the brochures and read.

Three surfers bobbed in the water as a 15 foot swell rolled in on the East Coast of Barbados. One of the surfers paddled into it, snapped to his feet and rode the wave, millions of gallons of the ocean's energy barreling him forward. He sped left, flipped right, then crouched down and held the sides of his board, launching himself five feet off the crest. He flew, spinning into the air, and landed with perfect ease on the wave, as it settled back down and drove into shore.

Clint had done things like this many times, had described the thrill of it to her, over and over. What went wrong with the wave he caught? Was there really a sudden riptide? Cindy was seized by a desire to read every single word that was written about Clint and how he died. There had to be some articles in the local papers. She made a note to check that out today.

Then she noticed another small brochure on the table next to her, a travel guide from a consulate in another country. Someone had left it there. An item caught her eye.

Visitor, sexually assaulted at knife point, life threatened and robbed in the middle of the day.

The police were indifferent. Locals outside of the tourist business confided that this was not surprising. She also read a consulate travel advisory warning of rape of tourists and increase in violent crime.

Cindy felt jarred. She'd had no idea about this, nor had she checked her consulate's travel warnings. She folded up the brochure and stuck it into her purse. Every scrap of evidence added to the picture.

The guy that had originally told her to wait came over, and pointed to a door down the hall. The secretary had returned from her break.

Cindy went to the door, opened it and walked in. There were only a few people milling around.

A lovely woman with sparkling eyes and pearl white teeth greeted her at the main desk.

"Welcome to Barbados," she smiled, incongruently. She seemed to take an instant liking to Cindy.

"I need a little information," Cindy said to the woman.

"Of course, dear, anything," the woman said.

"I'm looking for the original Coroner's report about my husband's death."

The woman looked up at her. "Oh my!"

"It happened a few months ago," Cindy said.

The woman shook her head. "I'm so sorry. Happened in Barbados?"

Cindy nodded.

"And to such a young woman."

The woman sighed. "Only God knows why he takes our loved ones from us."

Cindy wanted to stay on track. "The report we have in the US is a summary. It says accidental death, by drowning. I need more details."

The woman shook her head back and forth. "So much pain for such a beautiful young woman, like you."

Cindy was becoming frustrated. "I need more information about the investigation."

The woman shook her head again.

"What do you mean investigation? An accident is an accident. What is there to investigate? The surf can be dangerous on the East Coast. An investigation takes a long time here. First we have an inquest -" she sighed .

"I want the full Coroner's report." Cindy said more forcefully.

"We don't just release that."

"I just want to read it. You can make a copy of it. That's all I want."

"Yes, yes, I understand. But, we're very busy right now."

Cindy looked around. They didn't seem busy at all.

"It'll just take a minute. Isn't there some file with the reports?" she said.

"Of course there is a file," the woman said, "but you can't just come in and see it. We'd need identification and things like that."

"I have identification," Cindy said. "I came all the way from the United States alone to see the report."

The woman's eyes opened wide. "Alone?" That seemed to get to her. "Are you asking for an inquest?"

"No, I'm not," Cindy said. "I just want to compare your report and the one we have. See if we might have missed something."

"An inquest can take a couple of years," the woman said as if reading from a form. "We have to line up the witnesses, collect testimonies. The Coroner listens to the evidence."

Clearly, she wanted to discourage Cindy, send her away. That was her job. Those were her instructions. Cindy had to get around it.

" I don't want an inquest," Cindy repeated. "Believe me."

The woman's eyes glazed over.

"I'm all alone," Cindy said in a soft, trembly voice. "Woman to woman, I know you can help me. I just want to look at the report."

"Are you sure?"

Cindy bent close and touched her arm. "It'll only take a few minutes. Can't you give me a hand?"

Something in Cindy's tone touched the woman.

"Listen, sweetheart" she said, "I'll get the report and show it to you. I'll make you a copy, and that's it. We don't need any more trouble down here in Barbados."

Cindy was grateful . "That's great, that's fine. That's all I want."

"That's never all they want," said the woman. "And, what good is that gonna do? He died in Barbados. It's our jurisdiction. These

184

cases go on for years, and then nothing happens
. Let the dear man rest in peace and save
yourself a lot of tears."

Cindy didn't want to say that the killing may
have happened here in Barbados, but the crime
took place in the U.S. There was no need to go
into that with this woman.

"I miss my husband," Cindy said instead, "I
want to see what happened to him." Exhausted,
her voice was catching, almost on the verge of
tears.

"Okay, come on, don't you cry. I'll get that
report. It's not so difficult," the woman got up
and motioned for Cindy to follow her.

They walked to the back of the room and
then turned to walk down a narrow corridor.

"Rain's gonna whip up later," the woman
remarked as their footsteps sounded on the old,
wooden floor. Then she turned into a long,
narrow room, filled with huge filing cabinets
everywhere.

"Give me the name and the date."

"Clint Blaine. May 23, 2010."

"Recent," she murmured and ruffled
through the files. "You know, I think I heard
about that one. Died on his honeymoon?"

"Right," said Cindy.

"Okay," the woman said, ruffling through
each report quickly, expecting Clint's file to be
right there. It wasn't .

She paid more attention then, looked more slowly, carefully checking each name and date. Suddenly, she stopped and turned to Cindy.

"I can't find it anywhere."

"What are you talking about?"

The woman looked distressed, and turned back to check again.

"That's funny. We usually have a copy of everyone here."

A second go around brought up nothing.

"Someone must have taken it," the woman said.

"Who took it?" Cindy asked.

The woman had no idea.

"I just work at the front desk," she said in a sad, lilting tone. "I was trying to help you."

"Let me talk to the Coroner myself."

She looked at Cindy with a dead pan face. "Honey, he's a busy man. He's not going to talk to just anyone."

"I'm not just anyone. My husband was killed."

"I know and I'm sorry. But he's not available."

Cindy couldn't be angry with her. She was just doing her job and had done more than she was supposed to, anyway .

"Thank you for everything," Cindy said, turned and walked away.

"So sorry, so sorry, sweetheart," the woman called out. "Let him rest in peace. Let the island hold him. Let his spirit fly with our beautiful birds."

*

There was no doubt. The original report was hidden. There had to be a reason. It had to have been tampered with. Cindy had to confront the Coroner himself.

She knew the Coroner's office was in this building. He had to be a few steps away. She went to her car, opened her phone and checked out the Coroner's website to learn more about him.

His picture came right up. He was a prominent figure with a big, round face and smiling eyes.

Cindy immediately called his direct office and asked if he was in today.

The voice on the phone asked if she had an appointment. Cindy didn't, but needed one right away. The Coroner was in, but an appointment took three weeks to get, the person informed her. The Coroner was a very, very busy man.

Cindy didn't have time to wait. And she didn't have to. She would drive the car to the front of the building, sit there and wait for him to walk out. There was only one door he could exit from. The minute she saw him, she'd rush over and talk. How could he refuse her?

It seemed as if hours went by as she sat there in the heat, her eyes glued to the front path. She didn't turn on the air conditioner, as she wanted to be ready to jump out of the car the minute she saw him.

As Cindy waited, she wondered what her father would think if he saw her now? Cindy rarely thought of her father . She barely knew him; as she was growing up, he was so busy with his police duties. And she was so young when he died. But vague memories of him had been coming into her mind these past days. He was big and strapping and good natured. She'd always wanted to be strong like him. Would he be proud of her now? Or would he think she was crazy, subjecting herself to this ordeal?

As she was musing, Cindy suddenly saw the Coroner walking leisurely out of the building. She jumped out of the car and ran over to him.

"Mr. Kartrite," she said quickly, blocking his way.

He moved to the side, "Excuse me, miss," and kept walking.

Cindy slid beside him and walked at his side.

"I have to talk to you. It's important, urgent."

He kept walking and said nothing.

"I'm the wife of Clint Blaine," she continued. "The man who was killed on his honeymoon. I'm sure you heard."

"Please stop a minute and talk to me."

"I have an appointment."

"I need a copy of your report."

Cindy talked faster and faster and she walked beside him. "I have to compare your report to the one we received back home. A lot of terrible things have been happening since I got back to the U.S."

He stopped and looked at her. "What's a young lady like you coming here alone to find something like that?"

"I have no other choice. Please help me."

"There's nobody back home who could come and help you?"

Cindy shook her head.

He looked at her kindly, seemed to feel badly.

"It's not only my husband, my sister was hurt, my husband's friend killed."

The Coroner looked troubled.

"What can I do?" he said, flustered. "I told them everything I knew. They didn't listen. They changed the information."

"Oh my God," Cindy stopped moving. "Who?"

The Coroner stopped as well. They stared at each other.

"The report you have is not the one I wrote. It happens sometimes. Facts become inconvenient."

"I'm begging you to tell me what's in your report. I have to know."

"Your husband did not die from drowning," he finally said, sighing deeply.

Cindy's heart skipped a bit. She was afraid to ask.

"Then...of what?" she asked.

He stared at her. "He died from trauma to the head. And not from a surfboard."

Cindy felt herself trembling inwardly.

"From...what?" she asked, her voice almost a whisper.

"I couldn't say for sure. From the angle, though, I'd bet it was a speedboat. Run over."

Cindy felt physically sick. The image of it horrified her.

Still, finally, she had facts.

" I need the report and I need you to be a witness," she pleaded, tears filling her eyes.

He shook his head, and started walking away again.

She hurried to keep up with him.

"I cannot be a witness and I don't have the report. I just told you what I know. Let's keep it at that."

She grabbed his arm. "Please, it's not just him. My life is in danger. "

He grimaced. "Those rotten companies think they own the world."

"Yes," breathed Cindy.

"They think a few dollars in your pocket and they can do whatever they want."

"It's wrong," said Cindy.

"I know." He stood glued to the spot.

"Please," said Cindy heatedly, "you must have the report."

He nodded. "You promise that you will never tell them where it came from?"

"Never," Cindy vowed.

She gave him her card with her email address.

He stared at it, thinking. Finally, he relented.

"I'll email you. Pictures of the body, the medical examination, all of it," he suddenly said.

"Oh my God, thank you. Please, send it as soon as you can."

Without another word, he turned and hurried off to his car, jumped in, and sped off.

Cindy stood alone in the parking lot, wondering what to do next. She knew that she'd found what she'd come for, that she should just go quietly back home, wait for his email, and follow up with the FBI.

But a part of her could not let this go. She felt the need to press further, to hold everyone accountable. She could not just go quietly off into the night. That just wasn't her anymore.

The local police had clearly known. They had covered up the report. She needed to know who was paying them off. And she wouldn't rest until she did.

She knew it was foolish, but as she got back into her car, she knew that her next stop had to be the local police.

Chapter 22

Cindy was on a roll. She felt invincible. She'd been right all along, and now she had proof. Blunt trauma to the head. How dare someone hurt Clint like that? If it was the last thing she did in life, she'd find out who—and get justice.

Her body felt filled with wild energy as she drove down the road about half a mile to the police station.

Emboldened, Cindy walked in, as though she belonged. A crime had been committed and she'd be damned if she wasn't going to find out more.

"The Chief of Police," she said to the sleepy guy at the front desk.

He looked up at her for a minute and grinned. "Aint here, honey."

Cindy's skin crawled . "It's urgent. He's expecting me."

The guy laughed. "He's not expecting anybody. In fact this isn't even his office."

"Then where is his office?"

"La Moya. His favorite restaurant. "

"Where's la Moya?" Cindy asked.

The guy just shrugged.

Cindy moved closer to the desk, threateningly, "Look, this isn't a game," she said, her eyes flaring.

"Whoah, lady. Take it easy. Everyone knows la Moya's two blocks down the road."

Then he grinned again and closed his eyes. Cindy must have disturbed his nap.

Cindy got in the car and drove right to la Moya's.

It was a fancy restaurant, on the water, with a huge outdoor patio, lined with palm trees. People sat for hours on the patio, eating and drinking rum. Reggae music played in the background.

"The Police Chief's expecting me," she told the tall, thin waiter who greeted her. "Where is he?"

The waiter pointed to a table in the front. A huge man sat there, leaning back in his chair, drinking beer and eating.

"That's where he sits every day," the waiter said.

She went straight over to the Police Chief's table. "May I join you?"

He looked at her and laughed out loud. "Little tiger lady," he said, amused. "Sit down."

Cindy sat down opposite him. It was a beautiful spot, right near the water. How she wished Clint could be sitting here with her.

"Sorry to interrupt your lunch," she said.

He laughed out loud again, guffawed. He was a huge, muscular guy with big jowls and bags under his eyes. His teeth were tiny and yellow.

"Nobody interrupts my lunch," he said. "I eat all day long."

He was eating chewy conch fritters and delicately grilled flying fish fillets, along with a bottle of Barbados' brew, Banks beer. He stuffed a huge spoon of fritters into his mouth .

As she watched him eat, she let the rough, salty winds blow over her. It was so empowering to know that Clint had not died drowning, that she wasn't crazy, that her suspicions had a basis in fact. And that all her efforts were leading somewhere real.

"What can I do for the little lady?" he swallowed his mouthful loudly.

"My name is Cindy Blaine," she started.

It didn't mean a thing to him.

"My husband's name was Clint Blaine. He was killed in Barbados a short while ago."

Still no recognition.

"Killed on his honeymoon," Cindy continued, trying to get a flicker from him.

"Bad time to get killed," he said with a little jeer. "Of course there's no good time, but a honeymoon is about the worst of all."

Cindy felt completely repelled.

"Or maybe it was really a good time?" he went on. "Maybe he died after he got the best, and didn't have to go through the worst?"

Then he laughed again and stuffed more food into his mouth.

"I thought you might have heard of this case," Cindy tried her hardest to be professional.

That made him laugh even louder. He was enjoying every moment with her.

"Who he was, or why he did it, I have no idea. This island isn't forgiving," he suddenly looked grim. "I hear about killers all day long. Killing is natural down here, animals and people, eating each other up."

It was a horrible image. Cindy felt sick to her stomach.

"You know, lots of surfers come here and drown. People don't talk about it, but it happens all the time. We're used to it. These sweet, beautiful waves have a life of their own. You have to learn how to respect them, let them lead the way."

"Do you remember the case at all?" Cindy would not be sidetracked .

"How can I remember every case? So many cases we cover here. " He snorted. "To you the guy means something. To us, he's food for the fish."

Cindy blanched. There was no budging him in anyway .

"My husband was killed at the beach near El Barada Hotel."

He chewed on his lip a second. "You a detective?" he said.

"I'm a wife."

He barely heard what she said, put his fork down and looked out at the horizon, as if picturing the El Barada hotel.

"They like to blame the surf for every rotten thing that happens here on the island," he declared. "Your report probably said, riptide did it. Now I happen to love riptides. There's not one bad thing they can do to you. If you invade their territory, whose fault is it if you're dead?"

"Clint understood the ocean. He was a powerful surfer."

"Not powerful enough."

He closed his eyes a moment, and he started chewing on his lip again.

"There's plenty of ways to get yourself killed down here on the island. "

"I need information about the investigation," she persisted.

"You don't say? What kind of information?"

This was fun for him, a distraction in the afternoon. He was dangling her as though she were a little fish.

"Who found the body, who were the witnesses? It's strange that we didn't hear anything about them."

He made a sour face then, as if his lunch were repeating on him.

"To Americans everything is strange. Down here on the islands, everything is beautiful. Seems like you think you know a lot. But I'll tell you something you never thought of - someone dies because they're supposed to. If we say case closed, that's what it means. Go take up your grievance with God, not me."

"I'm not coming to you with a grievance," Cindy said. "I need to have some questions answered."

His big head bobbed up and down. "There are people who cannot accept reality. They'll fight it down to the last minute. Even get themselves killed doing it. I hope that's not you, tiger lady."

He pushed his plate back and motioned to the waiter. "Bring me another plate, another beer, and bring the same for the lady."

"I'm not hungry"

"You guys come down from the U.S. and think you're hot shots and we're a bunch of idiots that you can push around. Well, you guys got another thing coming. We used to be slaves but we're not anymore. We fought the battle for our independence, and we won. Barbados is an independent nation, even though we Bajans have more British flavor than any other island in the Caribbean. We're proud of our island, we're

197

proud of everything, and, we have more smarts than you."

He raised his hands to the sky as if he were preaching a sermon that was long overdue. The more he spoke, the more exhausted Cindy became and the more the sun seemed to beat down on her.

"This is our home and we love it," he went on. "We understand how the island twists and turns in funny ways. We know it's moods, hungers, disappointments, we take the beating of its storms." His voice was getting louder and louder. "We watch the animals that live off it . Some people, the island spits out. Others, it draws into its gut. Some it will never let go. Which one are you?"

He looked at Cindy with foggy, shifty, eyes.

The reggae music in the background was getting louder, as more people began filling in the tables for lunch. Cindy's head began to hurt.

He could ramble all he wanted. She wasn't going to let him throw her off course.

"I've seen the report," Cindy said, bluffing. "I've seen the Coroner's report. My husband didn't die from drowning. He died from trauma to the head. Someone falsified the findings."

She won. She caught him off guard for a second.

"I want the case re-opened," she added.

"When it's case closed, it's case closed," he said, scowling.

Cindy got it. The police had been paid off, not to investigate the case. It was clear as day. She suddenly became frightened about whether the Coroner would actually email her the report . Did he just say he would to get rid of her? She needed the report desperately.

She quickly opened her phone, under the table, to see if the email was there. Not yet. *Oh God*, Cindy, thought, *could this all be for nothing?*

"If I were you," the Police Chief went on, digging into a plate of rice and prawns, "I'd enjoy myself on the island of Barbados, take a vacation, relax in the sun. Go to the beach where your husband died, and say good bye to him. Then go back to your country and start again."

Then he put down his fork and took a huge gulp of beer.

"That's what you learn here on the island, how to start all over again. The waves teach you. They wash all kinds of stuff onto the beach and then they wash it away again."

Cindy couldn't bear listening to another word. The tone of his voice, smell of his food mixed with the hot sun was nauseating. She stood up to go.

"Thank you for everything," she started.

He didn't seem to want her to go. "Hey," he tried to stop her, "thought you were going to stay all night and keep me company. It can get pretty lonely down here once it gets dark."

Cindy shuddered.

"Who knows?" he grinned, "maybe if you stayed with me all the way until morning, I could find something to tell you?" He looked at her, questioning.

Sleep with him in exchange for information. Cindy would rather die. If she died, at least she'd meet up with Clint and this horrible charade would be done.

"Why don't you go drop dead," she said angrily, then stood up and stormed off.

She could hear him laughing behind her, his biggest laugh yet.

"Maybe I will, lady," he said. "But that ain't goin to bring your husband back, is it?"

Chapter 23

Cindy jumped back into her car and sped towards her hotel. Her mind raced, as she struggled to figure out who to talk to next. She couldn't go back home empty handed. She again tried to piece together everything that happened that final day with Clint. She remembered their breakfast, her nap…And suddenly, something came back to her: her waiter. His smile. That torte she served him. Could it have been poisoned? Could he have had something to do with it?

Cindy checked her email again. The report still wasn't there. The Coroner might still be out for lunch. She had to believe he wasn't lying, that it would arrive later.

She stepped on the gas, urging the small rental car to go faster. As she checked her rearview, she saw a police car a few blocks behind her, trailing her, and wondered if it could be following her. She drove faster.

When Cindy walked into the hotel, Alex was there behind the main desk, as he had been during the honeymoon. He looked up and greeted her warmly with a beautiful smile. It was time to let him know.

"Are you having a good day, Miss Cindy?" he asked.

Cindy went over and sat on a stool opposite him.

"Very good," Cindy said. Then she paused, "Alex."

"Yes, Miss?" he smiled lavishly.

"I came back down here for a reason."

His smile got stuck on his face.

His eyes opened wide. "What do you mean?"

"I need to find out more about what happened to my husband."

"Like what?" he seemed nervous.

"Anything I can find. His death wasn't an accident," she said bluntly.

"My God?" he looked startled. "You came down to stir up bad memories?" he opened both hands wide.

"I came down to find the truth."

"Down here on the islands, the truth has many faces," he flushed. "What do you want to do this for? What will you get out of it? I can tell you what the newspapers said, surfing accident - riptide came in. Surfers swim at their own risk here. I told you both as soon as you came in the door. New surfers go to Duncan Surfers School first, three miles down the road."

"He wasn't a new surfer."

"Even strong surfers get trapped in a wave. Especially in a riptide."

"Alex," she said,

Can you tell me the name of the waiter who served us lunch every day?"

The veins in Alex's neck bulged. "Why him?"

"The day Clint died, I got very sick after lunch. That's why I didn't go with him. It felt like food poisoning."

"Oh my God," said Alex.

"I just want to have a talk with the waiter."

"His name is Tomale," Alex said. "He's not working here anymore."

"Why?"

"He quit. The day you left."

She paused.

"Where can I find him?"

"He lives in a little town on the edge of the sugar cane fields. In a small house . He's a good man, takes care of his family. He's religious."

"Can you give me his address?"

Alex's eyes opened wide. "Of course not. You can't go to that neighborhood yourself."

Cindy reached out and touched his hand. "Please, Alex," she begged, "time is running out. They took my husband, but they can't take my spirit. I'm not living a life in fear."

Alex suddenly looked teary." I don't know why I'm doing this."

He gave her Tomale's address and directions to his home.

"It's not far from the U.S. Embassy," he said. "It's two miles up the road. "

"Back down, Miss Cindy, please. These are dangerous people. You think I could ever sleep at night if something else happened at my hotel? Especially to you?"

Alex genuinely cared about her and Cindy felt it.

"I'll always be grateful," Cindy said.

"I don't know if you will."

*

Cindy began driving fast along the bumpy roads which narrowed, twisted and led to the back part of the island. The road curved around a bend, wound in between clumps of tall, thin trees. This part of Barbados was a whole other world. It could have once been

the home of gigantic mythical creatures. Enormous limestone boulders were strewn in the shallows, as though giants played there and sat in the sun. The wind swept in relentlessly, the roads were hollowed and palm trees arched backwards, thinned by the howl of the wind.

As she turned off that road, she went deeper into the island, passing along high fields of sugar cane glistening in the setting sun. The fields went on as far as the eye could see, weaving gently back and forth, reaching towards the sky.. Small thatched roof cottages, and simple little houses dotted the fields. It was another world. Cindy was transported. She couldn't imagine what it would be life actually living here.

As she drove, she turned past the fields into a village, with small houses crowded next to one another, narrow alleys, the sound of voices calling, music playing, streets strewn with cans, bicycles, papers, laundry hanging on wires, and chickens running in the street. Tomale's house was one of these . It was getting harder to make out one house from another in the dimming light.

Cindy parked her car at the edge of a street and decided to walk. The air was cool and fragrant. A few stray children outside turned and looked at her as she went from house to house.

Finally, she found Tomale's, went up to the door and knocked.

A small, thin, frazzled man came to the door. Cindy remembered him clearly from the honeymoon. For a moment, he brought back beautiful memories, delicious lunches, long afternoon naps.

Tomale recognized her immediately. For a second, he was happy to see her again.

"Hello, Miss, hello. How are you?" Tomale had taken special notice of her and Clint on the honeymoon, always asking about their day.

Then, suddenly, it was different. "What you want? What you want?" he asked over and over, like a startled bird that had fallen from a tree.

"Can I come in?" Cindy said.

Tomale looked frightened. "Not now, not now."

"Tomale, please."

"Tomorrow," he could barely speak.

"Just for two minutes."

That soothed him. "Two minutes? Okay."

Inside, the place was dark, disheveled, heavy with the smell of beer. There were tiny, cracked windows. No one else was there.

"Everyone's gone," Tomale said, holding open both hands.

Cindy didn't know what he meant exactly.

"There's nothing here," he continued in a raspy tone.

He must have thought she came to check out his place, see if he was hiding anything.

"Tomale," Cindy said, "you remember my husband?"

He nodded quickly, overwrought. Then he turned away.

"He's dead."

Tomale began quivering. "I know, I know. But I didn't realize anything. I can't say anything else."

"Another person was killed back home too. And my sister was hurt. I could be next, Tomale."

He gasped. "Please believe me, I didn't realize anything."

"I'm not blaming you."

"Blame me," his head dropped.

"For what? You can make it all right again if you tell me."

He seemed to like that.

"I didn't mean anything, miss." He turned and faced her, tremblely. "My mother was dying. I didn't know what I was doing. I needed the money they gave me. Now she's gone anyway. You see," he motioned to the empty house. "She died two weeks ago."

"I'm very sorry."

"What did you do for them to give you the money?" Cindy asked.

"They said it was just to help you sleep. They gave me something to put in the afternoon torte. Just for you, *not* Mr. Clint."

"Food poisoning?"

"Not poison, a little something to make you sleep. They said they had to talk to him alone. I thought maybe they'd just rough him up a bit. That's all. I swear it!"

"Who said it?"

"The men from the U.S. God forgive me, am I making it all right now? Will God forgive me?"

"Tomale, will you come back to the U.S. with me and be a witness? I'll pay for everything. I'll give you extra for your family."

"There's no more family," he whimpered, "my mother is gone, everything is gone. When I found out that Mr. Clint was killed, I couldn't go to work anymore."

"Killed?" Cindy said. "You found that out?"

It seemed to be getting darker and darker outside, and the air in the house grew mustier as they spoke.

"God forgive me."

"How?"

"I had nothing to do with it. I promise you. I only found out later."

"How, Tomale?" she asked again, sweating in the small house.

Tomale shivered. A long silence filled the humid air.

"I heard that they ran over him with a boat. Head cracked open. "

Cindy crunched over in pain.

Suddenly, the sound of police sirens.

Tomale ran to the small window and peered out, petrified.

Cindy looked, too: three police cars were driving up to the house.

He looked over at her, his lip trembling. "Did you go to the police?" he asked her.

"Yes," she said.

"Oh my God," he said. "Why!? You have to run! Run away, hide!"

Waves of horror consumed Cindy. She couldn't move, was glued to the spot, as she watched the police cars stop and a bunch of policemen run up to the house and burst in .

One of them grabbed her around the waist. That woke her up. She tossed and turned, trying to loosen his grip. No matter what she did, it didn't make a difference. He was stronger, tougher. Her body felt frail beside him, like a twig that could snap at any moment. His face, which had sprawling, carved features, looked impassive and resigned. He'd probably done this a thousand times. Was he going to kill her? Now the thought of it made her both angry, and sad.

Was this it? Was she going to die? To her great amazement, she wasn't frightened. She almost felt ready.

At that moment, Tomale suddenly broke free, ran across the room, and kicked the policemen holding her, hard in the small of his back.

He cried out in pain and released her.

"RUN!" Tomale yelled at her, wide-eyed.

It was the last thing she heard, as she ran out the door. As she did, she saw them pouncing on Tomale in his house.

Under the shade of darkness she saw a motor scooter propped up against Tomale's picket fence. She jumped on, kicked back the starter, and screeched down the back road, Thank God Clint had taught her how to ride. She knew the U.S. Consulate was a couple of miles straight down. It wasn't far. She could make it. A huge, unexpected surge of energy filled her, as a loud rumbling sounded from behind.

She looked in the side mirror. Two police cars were on her trail. She revved the gas as far as it would go, and raced on and off the road, slipping between trees, around clumps of sugar cane. They couldn't follow her there. She slipped off the road and then back on again, over and over, heading straight in the direction of the Embassy.

As she got further, she heard the police cars closer.

Please God, just a little further. This is no way to die, on a back road in Barbados. There's too much good I can do alive.

Up ahead she could see the Embassy. Then, with one last, enormous push, she swerved off the road, on the road, and then straight through the Consulate gates.

Safe. Protected. On United States territory. The police could not follow her here.

She felt a vibration in her pocket and looked down at her cell phone. One new message. From the coroner. And it had attachments.

Chapter 24

When her plane landed at Kennedy airport, the word was out. Cindy was shocked. She was met by a flock of photographers and reporters. Cameras flashed. This was a big news story now.

As photographers flashed their cameras at her, she stood, stupefied, looking for the man supposed to meet her there: FBI Agent Farnell.

He was at the front of the gate, peering through the crowds, waiting for her.

He rushed forward to help her, making his way through the waves of people.

Before he got there, clusters of reporters ran up to Cindy, asking for comments.

"I'm happy to be home," was all she could say .

"Is there any other comment you have? When did you know DGB was implicated?"

"I'm not sure," Cindy was flustered.

"Did you know that the death of your husband would send a ripple all the way to Congress?"

Farnell put an arm around her and ushered her through the crowd into a waiting town car.

"What's going on?" said asked, stunned.

She felt as if she were in a crazy dream.

As the car took off and she settled comfortably, Farnell handed her a newspaper.

The headlines screamed: *Large oil company executive, Henry Greerson, arrested on suspicion of murder. Washington lobbyists and Congressmen possibly involved.*

Farnell looked at her with different eyes. "You did good."

"I didn't have a choice," said Cindy.

"Yes, you did."

"That coroner's report you sent me was just what we needed," he said. "We already have a confession from Greerson—he's looking to a plea deal. DGB is going to go down. And they're going to bring a lot of lobbyists—and a few Congressmen—down with them."

They drove in silence, getting onto the Van Wyck, heading in the direction of her house in Cove Bay.

"To be honest, I didn't think you could pull it off," he said, and broke into a small smile.

"I didn't think so, either," she said, smiling back.

"Want a job with the bureau?" he asked, smiling wide.

She looked at him and smiled back. "No thanks."

She finally set the paper down, closed her eyes, and breathed deeply. Flashes of Barbados kept crossing her mind.

"I faced death right on," Cindy said, "and I wasn't afraid. Do you know what that does to a person?"

"Yes," he said, as they drove in silence. "I do."

*

As Farnell dropped her off, she saw that Ann and Frank were waiting for her on her front lawn.

Ann's shoulder was in a sling, but she had a smile on her face. And Frank, for the first time, smiled back at her, too. He looked at her with a whole new respect.

Ann ran up, and the two of them embraced. They both started to cry.

"I'm so happy you're well," Cindy said.

"And I'm so happy you're home safe," Ann said.

As they pulled away and headed towards the house, Frank looked at her.

"I'm sorry, Cindy," he said, "for everything I said. It seems you were right all along."

He put a protective hand on her shoulder as he lead them into the house.

*

Hours later, the three of them still sat around the kitchen table, drinking coffee, watching the news, and going over the story endlessly. Finally, they were getting tired out. And it was almost time for Ann and Frank to go. For good, this time.

"Clint's family called," Ann said.

Cindy's body clenched up.

"Don't worry. They've changed their tune. They've seen the news. They're actually grateful to you. They're relieved to know how he died. They're grateful for everything you've done. And I think they're ashamed of themselves. They don't know how to thank you."

"I don't need them to thank me," Cindy said. "I'm content."

"Well, at least they've dropped the whole house issue. They said to tell you that it's yours to keep. They're not going to try to fight you on it."

Cindy nodded. She looked around the place and realized how much it felt like home. She was happy she wouldn't have to leave it.

*

The next morning Cindy woke up alone in the house, and for the first time, she felt good. It was different now being home in Cove Bay. She jumped out of bed, and began her day. She was grateful to be here for now. There was still a lot of cleaning to do, especially from the mess from the break in, and Cindy was happy to do it. She wanted to put everything in order, make the place a home again.

She got up and went to the window. Summer was here and the garden was in full bloom. She opened the window and leaned out, letting the fragrance of the flowers and trees fill her.

She walked out of the house and into the garden that she and Clint had started. It was beautiful, filled with color and life. As she stood there, among the flowers they'd planted, she knew that Clint was with her, and that he would have wanted her to let her life bloom, too.

As she stood there, staring, her cell phone rang. She kept the ringer on these days, and she was no longer afraid to answer it.

It was Helene. An old college friend, from Wisconsin. She'd read about what had happened to Clint, and what Cindy had accomplished in Barbados. Helene was amazed. She said that she, herself, had been living on a Caribbean Island for the past six months. But something awful had happened. She couldn't tell Cindy what over the phone. Her voice started to shake.

Cindy held her breath. She felt Helene's anguish.

Helene had already called in two Private Investigators, but it hadn't do any good. She needed help badly. Would Cindy help her? She didn't know where else to turn. She would pay a good fee and all expenses if Cindy would only fly down and help.

"I'm not a detective," said Cindy.

"Please," Helene said. "I don't know who else to ask. I'm at a dead end. And you've been through this. You understand what I'm going through. And clearly you know what you're doing."

Cindy thought of her father. Was he looking down, trying to push her, still, to follow in his footsteps?

"Let me think about it," Cindy said.

She took down all of her information before hanging up.

She closed her eyes and breathed deep, listening to the call of the summer birds. Maybe this had all happened for a reason. Maybe she could help others, too.

Maybe, just maybe, she'd go.

COMING SOON...
Book #2 in the Caribbean Murder Series

To join the mailing list and be notified of future books, please email: jadenskyeauthor@gmail.com

Please visit Jaden's site, where you can hear the latest news about the novels, and find links to follow Jaden on Facebook, Twitter, Goodreads and elsewhere: www.jadenskye.com